Time On Her Hands

Annette Towler

One

Molly looks in the mirror and pulls a face, noting the slight wrinkles on her forehead. She smiles to herself realizing that she needs to get used to being in her sixties. She looks in the mirror again and appreciates that despite the moments of vanity, she looks good for her age. Her hands move over her body, taut from strenuous exercise and stretching. The firm muscles in her legs denote a love for running. Molly takes out her eyeshadow and applies the purple shade to her lids. She stands back from the mirror and looks at the effect, realizing that she doesn't wear make-up frequently. She turns around and looks at the dress on the bed. The dress is tight at the top to show her slim figure and flares at the bottom to show the glamor of the night. Because tonight there is a party for Molly at the university. It is time for Molly to say goodbye to academic life. The phone rings and Molly rushes to answer it, hoping it is someone she knows. She laughs when the automated voice offers another car warranty. She takes a breath and looks at the dress again.

"You are a good-looking woman Molly," she says out loud, because she is nervous.

She picks up the dress and steps into it, hoping it zips up properly because she has never felt entirely comfortable wearing luxury clothing. She faces herself in the mirror and smiles again because the dress suits her. She is glad that she listened to the sales assistant, who recommended a dress to suit a younger woman. Molly's fair hair frames her face, and she pulls the curling tongues out of the drawer and plugs it into the socket. She looks at herself in the mirror again, waiting for the tongues to heat.

"You've come a long way from England," she says to herself again, thinking about her parents and how they would have been proud if they were still alive. Raised in a small village on the border of England and North Wales, Molly had led a simple life growing up. Her life had changed when she met Michael, and she had fallen in love for the first time. Only tonight, he wasn't around. He was busy again at the hospital, still in demand as a doctor. She sighs, thinking of all the events he has missed yet somehow, he has stayed faithful to her, not engaging in the antics of an amorous doctor.

Molly glances in the mirror again just to remind herself that she is still a pretty woman from England. A woman who takes care of herself. A friend once told her that she was the full package, and she liked to think that she had tried to do her best as a college professor. Her phone emits its usual ping, and she realizes that the driver is outside. She grabs her bag and pulls her mask over her face, wondering how long it will continue. Less than twenty people are expected at the party and the university protocol expects a mask, even for those who are vaccinated. Careful not to smear her lipstick, she places the KN95 protective mask on her face, glad for the snugness that it provides. She opens the front door of the house and smiles at the driver when she gets into the back of the car. The driver says the destination, and she smiles at him and confirms the place: the chair of the psychology department booked a room in the university, and it is close to the student union on Kenwood Boulevard.

"Are you a professor?" asks the driver and Molly guesses from his accent and appearance that he is from India or Pakistan.

"I was. This is my retirement party," says Molly.

"But you aren't from America. English?"

Molly nods and confirms the driver's guess at her nationality. She slides back against the seat, thinking of how she arrived in America as a twenty-four-year-old, looking to gain a graduate education. She gained all the qualifications graduating with a PhD and getting tenure at the university, rising to the rank of full professor. Yet somehow, she still feels like the child who ran across the fields. The driver parks outside the building and Molly tips him generously. Ever punctual, she glances at her watch to make sure she has time to climb the stairs without feeling anxious. Having faked extroversion at various functions, she is used to wearing a social crown. She walks into the room, and a host of faces greet her. She sees one of the other retirees enjoying a glass of red wine.

"Is that pinot Betty?" asks Molly.

Betty smiles and kisses Molly on the cheek.

"I'm taking the pinot and the package," says Betty.

"It was hard to resist,' says Molly, as she asks the server for a glass of chardonnay.

"I'm in the mood for white tonight," says Molly, "the start of something new."

"Well, yes," says Betty, "you have a book to write. How's the first draft coming along?"

"Quite well," says Molly, "I like my detective. He's not Poirot but he has class."

More people gather in the room to say farewell to those who have retired. There are five faculty who will not be returning in the Fall: all of them have chosen to take the premium retirement package. The department chair makes a speech and thanks the retirees for all their hard work. Molly looks around the room and realizes that she will miss her colleagues. One of the younger faculty walks over to her and whispers in her ear.

"You are getting out at the right time. There's a freeze on hiring tenure-track faculty. They are relying on adjuncts."

Molly pulls a face and thinks back to the previous year realizing that her colleague is right. He whispers again in her ear.

"It will be virtual in a few years."

"Even after the pandemic is over?" asks Molly.

Her colleague nods and Molly feels sad.

"That's too bad," she says.

Molly looks around the room again and the crowd is thinning. She feels the sadness in her body because despite the anticipation of a fresh start, there is something inside her that feels the loss. She walks around the room and whispers goodbye to her former colleagues. She walks over to Betty and hugs her.

"Make sure you call me," says Betty.

"I will," says Molly, realizing that the decades at the university are over. She takes the phone out of her bag and calls the driver to pick her up. She walks outside to clear her mind and waits for the driver to arrive. At the steps, she turns around and looks back at the building. It is a leap of faith yet somehow it feels like the right path for her. The job had become a convenient place to work rather than a source of pleasure. She feels the mixture of loss and happiness sweep across her body and rather than push it to one side, she lets the feelings dance around, acknowledging each of them. She has helped the university for a long time.

"It's your turn," she says to herself, and laughs at the cliché. She turns back and the driver is waiting for her. It is eleven at night when the driver drops her back at the house and she gives him a tip. The house is dark, and she tiptoes upstairs to the main bedroom. She creeps into the bathroom, takes off her dress and removes her make-up, grateful to close the bathroom door and switch on the light. Once done, she switches off the bathroom light and tries to find her way to the bed, carefully touching familiar objects like the chest of drawers so she doesn't lose her balance. She slides into the bed and reaches out to touch Michael, but he isn't there. Startled, she switches on the bedside lamp. She can't believe Michael isn't at home in bed. In all the years they have been together, he always comes home from work, even if it is in the early hours of the morning. He has always been fixated with time. Molly is wide awake now, panic coursing through her body considering all the various scenarios. She takes a deep breath, trying not to panic and she walks down the stairs to pick up her cellphone, trying to remember his number. By now, the house is illuminated with light and the adrenaline is pumping through Molly's body. She finds her cellphone in her bag and scrolls through the list of contacts, quickly finding Michael's number. The phone rings and there is no answer, and there is a quick switch to voicemail after a couple of minutes.

"What am I doing?" says Molly, and her words echo around the house.

She takes another breath and sends Michael a text, trying to stay calm while feeling the rising panic inside her. She sends the text.

"Where are you?"

There is no response so Molly phones the main desk at the

hospital and her heart is beating so fast she can hardly bear to hear it. It seems like an eternity until someone answers the phone and the operator transfers her to Michael's department. Molly speaks to the nurse on duty and voices her concern.

"He is normally home before ten. I'm quite worried."

The nurse tells Molly she will look in Michael's office to see if he is working late and Molly holds her breath, frightened that he will be found on the office floor.

"He's not in his office," says the nurse, "I wonder where he is. I'm sure he is on his way home to you."

"I hope so," says Molly, taking a breath, "I'm sure you are right."

Molly thanks the nurse and stands in the hallway, frozen, unsure of what to do. She texts Michael one more time, feeling desperate.

"I'm worried. I hope you are fine."

Her hands are shaking, and she walks into the kitchen and picks up the electric kettle, her customary morning routine. Only this time, it is the early hours of the morning, and she feels like a robot unable to understand what has happened. She puts water into the kettle and listens to it boil. The act of standing in place wakes her up and she shakes her head.

"I am an idiot," she says to herself. "I can't think straight."

She picks up the phone again and calls the local police station to find out if there's been an accident, the worse-case scenario flooding her mind with thoughts of a head-on collision with another car with Michael unable to swerve and a street filled with broken glass.

She pushes the thought out of her mind and walks into the living room with the cup of tea in her hand. She sips the tea, feeling the warmth of the tannins move down her throat: she starts to relax.

Her eyes start to close, and she stretches out on the couch, waiting and hoping for the door to open. Tiredness overwhelms her and sleep enters her body, yielding no resistance.

A few hours later, she wakes up and light is seeping into the living room. Michael is not at home. Molly looks at her phone and checks the messages but there is nothing from her husband and no calls from the hospital. She sighs, realizing that the situation is out of her control. It is six in the morning and her daughters are getting ready for work. Molly's daughters are both busy professionals, so she picks up the phone choosing to call the eldest first. Sarah answers the phone straight away.

"What is it mom?" asks Sarah, in her distinct mid-west accent, a beautiful contrast to Molly's English tones.

"It's your dad. He didn't come home last night. I need to call your sister, but I just wanted you to know."

"What happened?"

"I don't know. I've called the police and the hospital. There's no report of an accident."

"Shall I come over?

"No, you've got work. And we still need to limit contact. If you hear from your father, just let me know."

"I will. I wish I could help you. I'm working virtually today. Sam's test came back negative so we should be able to see you in a few days once he gets the second test result."

"I'm sure it's frustrating for you both. I'll let you know once I hear something."

Next on the list is Molly's younger daughter, Emily, whose occupation and lifestyle have often left Molly feeling confused and naïve. She looks at her watch, unsure if Emily will be awake given her nightly flings. Throwing caution to the wind, Molly phones Emily. It's seven o-clock in the morning and she can tell when Emily answers the phone that she has had a late night.

"Sorry for ringing you so early honey," says Molly, unconscientiously breaking into American language that long evaded her.

"I'm still in bed," says Emily.

"Oh," says Molly, "I didn't realize."

There is a silence that swamps the phone line. Emily stretches out of her slumber and looks at the body next to her.

The man, whoever he is, is still asleep. Emily, who needs coffee, wipes her eyes and looks at the man again because it was a good night.

"Hey mom, I'll call you back in five minutes, okay. I need to get some coffee."

"Yes, please do," says Molly, "It's important. Your dad is missing."

"What? Missing?"

"Yes. Can you just check your phone to see if he contacted you?"

"I'll call back. I need some coffee."

Emily jumps out of bed, ignoring the man who is still sleeping. Quickly, she glances back at him and heads to the kitchen to make an espresso. She looks at the kitchen clock, seeing that it is late. She is not due to meet the client until eleven, but she realizes she needs to get ready and ask the man, whoever he is, to leave. She tries to remember his name. She pops a pod inside the machine and pours water into the top, waiting for it to boil. It is quick and she quickly gulps the coffee down feeling the caffeine surge through her body and waking her up. She scrolls the messages on her phone but there are none from her father, so she phones Molly.

"Nothing from dad," she says, hearing her mother sigh and she thinks of the man who is still in her bedroom.

"I'll let you know if I get any messages," says Emily.

Emily returns to the bedroom and touches the man on his shoulder.

"I've made you a coffee," she says and hands him a cup, full of espresso.

"Thanks Emily," he says, and Emily curses herself because

she still can't remember his name.

"I need to get ready for work," she says, watching the man drain the coffee from the cup.

She stands for a moment with her hands on her hips and looks at him, with no suggestion of intimacy.

"You know I like you, Emily."

"Yes, I know. I like you too. It's just that I have a rule."

"I know you told me. No entanglements. I hoped you might change your mind."

Emily shakes her head, wishing that for once she might throw caution to the wind and run off with one of the strangers in the bed. Especially with this one, because he is very good-looking. But today is not that day so she bids farewell to her one-night lover, gets into the shower and the water from the jets hits her body, like a series of small darts. It feels like a punishment.

Two

It is almost noon and Molly has exhausted all her options. She has phoned the hospital, the police, and local friends of Michael. Nobody has heard from him. When the phone rings just after noon, Molly jumps because the house has been silent since Michael's disappearance.

"Hello," says Molly, with a tinge of fear in her voice.

"I need to speak to Molly. Molly Williams."

"This is Dr. Williams."

"This is Sergeant Brown from the Highland Police Department".

"Highland?"

"We are in Indiana. We have your husband with us."

"Is he in trouble?"

"No. He's just a little confused. You need to come and collect him. He asked for you."

Sergeant Brown gives Molly the address and she writes it down, with relief entering her body yet also concern about Michael's state of mind. She wonders what the sergeant meant in describing Michael as a little confused.

Pushing the thoughts from her mind, she gets in the car, using the navigating system so she can reach Highland, Indiana in a reasonable amount of time. She is about to start the engine when the phone rings again and she recognizes the Highland number.

"Dr. Williams. It's Sergeant Brown again. After I spoke with you, I told your husband about our conversation. The thing is that he's left the station. I tried to catch him, but he was too fast for me. He said he was going home to see you."

"Did he do something wrong?" asks Molly, "I don't understand why you kept him."

"We don't plan to charge him with anything."

Molly hears the hesitancy in the sergeant's voice, and she wonders what has happened. She looks at her watch realizing that Michael will get home in a couple of hours. Molly thanks the sergeant and ends the call.

She looks at the phone for a moment unsure of what to do and she gazes down the hallway and looks in the living room, almost wanting Michael to appear but there isn't anyone there. There is just the sound of her breathing.

Molly touches her forehead, and it is moist. She is sweating, and the events of the last twenty-four hours come back. Her body swells up and she feels fatigued. She shakes her head trying to snap out of the feeling and massages her neck trying to ease the tension. She takes a breath and calls her daughters. Neither of them answers the phone so she leaves a short message to tell them that their father is safe. Molly hesitates to leave an explanation because she is unsure what is wrong. Most importantly, she has a terrible feeling that something is wrong with Michael. It is unlike him to be dazed or to break rules and protocol.

Grasping onto normalcy, Molly walks into the kitchen and pours water into the electric kettle. Her mother always said that tea was the healing liquid.

Once the water is boiled, she pours the fluid into a cup and dips the teabag into the water, waiting for it to ferment. She waits a few moments and once it is ready, she takes the teabag out of the cup and walks into the living room, unsure of what to do. The one thing she knows she must do is not to leave. She must wait for Michael to return.

She closes her eyes and imagines him driving down the highway safely. She has no other choice but to stay calm. This time she is wide awake when she hears the door open and she glances at her watch, knowing that Michael has arrived sooner than she expected. He walks into the living room, and she rushes to him.

"I was worried," she says, running into his open-stretched arms. She hugs him tight, knowing that something is wrong. He looks at her with an energy in his eyes that she has never seen before. She doesn't recognize him.

"What happened Michael?" she says.

"I am full of life," he says, and he grabs hold of Molly and thrusts her into the air. She laughs for a moment, feeling the strength in his hands. He lowers her down and kisses her with a passion that reminds her of the time when they first met.

"Let's dress up," he says and grabbing her hand, he pulls her towards him. Michael runs up the stairs and disappears into the main bedroom. Buoyed by Michael's enthusiasm, she jogs up the steps, feeling a mixture of emotions.

She discovers Michael searching through drawers, tossing T-shirts and trousers onto the floor. Michael holds up a t-shirt that is several years old.

"Look what I've found Molly," he says, holding up the t-shirt with a picture of Debbie Harry sprayed across the top.

Molly laughs at the sight of one of her favorite singers. She watches Michael struggling to put on the t-shirt over his head, so she goes over to help him.

"I can do it," says Michael, still revving with enthusiasm.

Molly backs away, watching him pull the t-shirt over his casual top, which is more modern in style. Michael gazes in the mirror and looks at himself. The t-shirt is at odds with his body. He is now in his sixties and the excess of food and too little exercise have taken their toll.

"Look at me!" he says in delight, "I can get any woman that I want."

He turns towards Molly, and she sees the look of delight light up his face.

"What happened?" says Molly, "This isn't you."

Michael looks at himself in the mirror again and turns towards Molly.

"Yes, any woman Molly. I can get any woman."

Michael rushes past Molly and down the stairs and Molly runs after him wondering what he is going to do next. She finds him at the bottom of the stairs searching through the shoes.

"Michael, what are you doing?"

"I want to run. Come with me Molly. Come with me."

There is a look of glee in Michael's face and Molly knows that he is having an episode because she has seen this happen with so many clients over the years.

It isn't Michael and the idea of him being with other women makes her embarrassed and deeply ashamed. Having lived with him for decades, she knows that faithfulness is central to his character.

Feeling pressured yet also exhilarated by his air of jollity, she spots her running shoes under the hallway bench and puts them on, grateful that she is wearing her active clothing. She laces up her shoes and stands up, realizing it is too late to stop Michael.

He is too quick for her, and despite his lack of exercise, he zooms out of the house with the zest of a much younger man. And all the while, the voice in Molly's head is telling her that Michael is having an episode, and it has arrived out of nowhere.

She runs out of the house and the voice is still gripping her thoughts and she tries to ignore the self-talk, but she thinks of all the times that Michael was moody and all the times when he acted like a child. It seems so obvious now in retrospect and yet it was easy to ignore the small signs of helplessness. Only now, Molly is running into something that is so large and obvious, it can't be swept away. Molly looks ahead and she is catching him up. There was never any competition between them when it came to running. Occasionally, when they were younger, he joined her on her easy runs yet even those were difficult for him, especially after the weight gains. Now, Michael is flying down the street like an athlete at the top of his game, full of adrenaline and although Molly is gaining ground, he eludes her. Michael runs past the four lions of upper east side, past the lighthouse, and onto the path that surrounds Lake Park. Molly gains ground and finally catches up with him. Michael is panting and the sweat from the exertion of the running is pouring down his face.

"Please stop Michael," says Molly.

He looks at her for a moment in a daze and stops in his tracks trying to work out what has happened.

Michael's breath is heavy, and Molly grips his arm to help him stay steady. She spots a bench in the park and steers him over to sit down.

"I don't feel well," says Michael and he slumps on the bench, closing his eyes to rest. Molly searches her pockets to find the cellphone, relieved that she has brought it with her, despite the mad dash from the house to the park.

"Take deep breaths Michael. I'm calling an ambulance."

Michael is exhausted and doesn't protest because the pain in his chest is getting worse.

"My chest," he says, "I feel sick."

Molly dials 911 and tells them the location.

"Please hurry," she says, "My husband. I think he's having a heart attack."

She looks at her watch, pleading for the ambulance to arrive soon. She keeps a grasp on Michael's hand, and she can see that he is losing consciousness, and she grips his hand even tighter. He doesn't say a word. Within ten minutes, they arrive although it seems like an eternity to Molly, who is also in shock because she feels that she is losing her husband.

The medical technician straps Michael onto the gurney and moves him into the ambulance. Molly climbs into the ambulance and takes a seat close to the door, feeling helpless. She looks at the two technicians and snaps out of the shock, because they are doing everything to save Michael. The mask that she is so careful to put on her face is forgotten in her pocket.

"His pulse is shallow," says one of the emergency technicians and he reaches for the defibrillator.

"What's happened?" asks Molly

"His heart. We need to try and resuscitate him," says one of the technicians.

In shock, Molly realizes that Michael's heart has stopped, and she watches as the technicians try to get his heart beating again. Slowly, his heartbeat returns but it is slow, and the technicians keep trying to revive him. By the time they reach the hospital, it is over. The two technicians shake their heads and look at Molly, who is unable to speak. She shakes her head.

"Thank you for trying to save him," she says.

Molly is faced with the reality that her husband has gone. The technicians take her into the hospital, aware that Molly is in shock, and they call one of the nurses to help her.

"I need to call my daughters,' says Molly, trying to function yet in a daze.

"Shall I do it for you?" asks the nurse.

Molly shakes her head coming out of her daze and snapping back into some semblance of reality, even if she is not fully aware. She calls Sarah with the thoughts in her mind zooming around and with her heart racing.

"Sarah," she says, her voice trailing off.

"What happened mom? Is it dad? Is he ok?"

"He collapsed in the park. I called the ambulance, and they tried to resuscitate him."

Molly stutters and can't find the words.

"Is he dead mom?"

"Yes. I'm so sorry," says Molly and she listens to her daughter weeping on the phone, waiting for her own tears to arrive but they don't come.

"I need to call Emily. She doesn't know," says Molly, who is shocked and dazed.

Molly snaps back into action and phones Emily but the call goes straight to voice mail because Emily is in a late meeting with a new client.

"Please call me Emily. It's urgent," says Molly, the signs of fatigue showing in her voice. She is very tired and looks at the nurse, finally wanting some support.

"Can I get you something to help you? Some medication?"

"I just want to go home," says Molly, "I'm not one for taking pills."

"I'll arrange for transportation," says the nurse and Molly thanks her, appreciative that finally she can go home and try to deal with the mess of the day. The driver arrives and she steps into the vehicle, choosing the back seat. The driver doesn't speak, and Molly sighs and the voice in her head is saying "what about you Molly? What about you? What mess did you make?"

It is a short drive back to the house and the driver gets out of the vehicle to help Molly because he can see that she is shaken even though he doesn't know what has happened to her. He doesn't need to ask because the pain is etched on her face. Despite the strength in her body, Molly feels like an old woman and when the driver reaches out his hand to help her down the steps from the vehicle, she takes it without hesitation. She smiles and thanks him, aware that she is in denial and still hasn't cried any tears for Michael. Because how can you explain to the world that the feelings are mixed and complicated? She pauses for a moment before entering the house, wanting to say something to the driver.

"We were married for almost thirty years," she says.

"A long time," says the driver.

And the voice in Molly's head is still spinning and she wants the ugly voice to go away: "But you didn't know him, Molly. You didn't really know him." She gets the keys out of her running jacket, glad that they weren't lost in the park due to the maelstrom of events. She tries to push the thoughts out of her mind, yet they keep coming, almost attacking her with their fury. When Molly's cellphone rings, she is startled because she was distracted by all the mayhem and still, she is aware that she hasn't cried. It is her younger daughter, Emily who has just finished the session with her client and has checked her cellphone messages to see the urgent one from Molly. Being a lawyer, Emily's brain connects the dots automatically and she realizes the news before her mother tells her.

"It's dad, isn't it?" she says, when her mother answers the phone.

"I'm sorry Emily. He's gone."

"That's too bad," says Emily and the tears stream down her face. Molly hears her daughter sobbing, and she doesn't know what to do. Emily shakes her head and thinks of her mother.

"I'm so sorry Mom," she says, "I love you."

And finally, the tears flow down Molly's face, and she grips the table, trying to steady herself. The silence is unbearable to Molly, yet she doesn't know what to say until she remembers that she is the organizer, always willing to set the table and cook the food. She tells her daughter what she needs.

"I'll come over tonight, after work," says Emily.

"You sister is coming too. We can work out what to do," says Molly, glad to play the organizer although she knows that she is putting on an act to protect her daughters. She walks up the stairs into the bedroom and looks at Michael's clothes, neatly hung up in his section of the walk-in wardrobe. Michael was methodical in his taste, choosing shirts with starched collars and shoes that he liked to get shoe-shined every Friday. Molly looks at her own casual outfit and feels unkempt, so she takes off all the athletic clothes and gets into the shower. It is only when the water hits her body in angry bursts does she cry again. Because he has gone, and she doesn't know what to do.

Three

An hour after Molly has arrived back at the house, her daughters arrive, and they hold each other. Molly grips her daughters so close; it is almost painful. The pain of the loss is hitting her. She breathes and tells them the plan.

"Father Tom called me," says Molly, "The service is at St. Mary's. He's coming tomorrow to discuss the arrangements. It will be on Friday. The service."

"What happened Mom? What happened to dad?" asks Sarah.

"After he got home, he wanted to go for a run. When he stopped running, he felt weak and so I called the ambulance."

"A run?" asks Emily, "that's not like dad. I've never seen him running."

"He ran a little when he was young," says Molly, wondering if she should tell her daughters what really happened.

"I don't understand how he ended up in Indiana," says Emily. Sarah, the eldest daughter, has nothing to say and her eyes are filled with tears. Sarah has always been the sentimental one in the family.

"I think he had an episode," says Molly, knowing she can't stop the truth from coming out. Eventually, her daughters will have worked it out because they are both intelligent women in high-paying careers.

"What do you mean Mom?" says Sarah, "An episode. That sounds like mental illness."

"Is dad Bipolar?" asks Emily, who has seen all types of behavior in her job as a family lawyer.

"But he was never diagnosed," says Sarah, whose brow is furrowed at the thought of her father struggling for years with an illness that nobody knew about.

"Well, he did get moody at times," says Emily and Molly remembers the times when he shut himself off refusing to make amends after an argument. The arguments that their daughters did not know about. The two daughters look at their mother.

"Did you know mom?" asks Sarah.

"Well, I'm a clinician so I did see the signs."

Molly looks at her two daughters, realizing they are hoping for an explanation, but she doesn't know what to say to them. "I didn't really know," she says. "It was only when he came back from Indiana that I realized what had happened. It can stay hidden for years until there is a breakdown."

"Can I get you something mom?" asks Sarah and Molly shakes her head.

"I feel useless," says Molly, "I need to do something. Let's make some tea."

"Let us do it," says Emily, spotting the tiredness around Molly's eyes. It's been a long and draining day for all of them, especially her mother who is still in a state of shock, not really acknowledging that her husband has gone. Normally efficient in conquering household chores, Molly sinks back into the sofa and touches her hands to make sure that she is still real because everything seems like a movie from one of the great directors with her daughters as the stars of the film.

Her racing mind collapses, and she closes her eyes, her body closing in on her. She touches her hands again and wakes up to the knowledge that Michael is gone yet her daughters are here. It is all that she has. Molly's daughters bring in a tray filled with cups and Molly looks at the teapot, which has been idle for several months.

Typically, she brings it out for special occasions such as birthdays. Sarah places the tray on the table and Emily pours the hot fluid into the cups. Molly looks down at her hands again, wanting to hold the cup of tea yet unsure of what to do. They all need a cup of tea. Emily hands Molly a cup and Emily's brow furrows as she dips into her pocket to stop the buzzing. A grin spreads across Emily's face, and she notices her mother looking at her.

"It's just some guy. I've stopped seeing all the others," says Emily.

"I'm guessing Covid got us all," says Molly, realizing that her daughter is embarrassed. Molly looks at Sarah to see her response, but Sarah appears clueless about her sister's love life. In fact, it seems that Sarah doesn't seem interested and is more intent on serving tea to her mother. However, Molly can't help but notice that Sarah is very nervous when she pours the tea. It is in the execution of little things where trauma resides.

"How is Sam?" asks Molly.

"Busy, as usual. But happy," says Sarah, and Molly detects the strain in her face, and she wonders what has happened.

Sarah and Sam have been married for five years and it was a brief engagement. They always seemed so happy to Molly, and it is only recently that she has noticed a change in Sarah when she speaks of Sam. And all the while she is thinking about her daughter, she is also hearing the persistent voice of the critic calling to her. "What are you thinking? He's dead. He's dead. Your husband has gone, you fool."

The three women sip the tea from the cups and Emily shatters the polite conversation.

"I can't believe he has gone," she says.

In that moment, the three women cry together, and the reality hits them that a central figure in their life has gone. Gone within a day and it doesn't get worse than that.

"It's his age too," says Sarah, "He was too young."

"I'm glad his parents aren't alive to see this," says Molly, "It would have crippled his mother."

And they weep again, holding each other and dismissing the teacups as mere intrusions into their grief. Eventually, Molly looks at the clock and it is getting late.

"You both need to go and rest," she says.

"Do you want us here tomorrow?" asks Sarah.

Molly shakes her head.

"I just need to talk with Father Tom. He will explain what will happen. The catholic service is full of rules and protocol. I'll call you both and tell you the time of the service. You can come with me to the funeral. I don't want to do that alone."

"Of course, Mom" says Sarah.

"We'll both be there," says Emily, thinking of her lover who is waiting for her at the bar.

Molly watches the two of them leave the house and she realizes she is alone. Alone for the first time in years because solitude is the antithesis of loneliness. It feels strange and uncomfortable to her because she lived with Michael for so long. She takes the tray full of cups into the kitchen and opens the refrigerator, pleased to see the half-finished bottle of Chardonnay in the fridge. She needs something to ease the pain in her heart.

"Just one glass," she says to herself as she pours the liquid into one of the wine glasses.

She takes the glass into the living room and sits on a favorite chair. Placing her feet on the ottoman, she sips from the glass and savors the rich aromas of fruit. It is an expensive bottle of wine, to be enjoyed.

She sips from the wine, feeling peace flow from her body into her weary mind and as she continues to savor the wine, the critical voice from the past stops its weary banter. It doesn't take long until Molly's eyes start to close, and she dozes and sinks into the comfortable chair, thinking about her daughters and how they help her in so many ways. There is also a little of her inside them both. In their own ways, her two daughters have a rebel streak.

In the downtown bar, Emily is sitting on a stool looking at her lover and wondering if she should take a risk with him because she likes the way he looks at her. It is a little more meaningful than the other ones.

"I'm glad you called me," says Ryan.

By now, Emily has remembered his name. It also helped that she found his business card inside her wallet so was able to hide the embarrassment through feigning recognition when they met again. It is rare for Emily to go on a second date. She also remembers that he has been vaccinated so there is no need for a mask, which is how she likes it.

She looks down at Ryan's hand that is strategically placed on her inner thigh. Emily smiles and feels a softness inside her body with the knowledge that he wants her. She looks down at her body, mindful that a small community of men like women who are on the large side. As if he is reading her mind, Ryan leans over and whispers in her ear.

"I love your body. I want you."

Emily leans over and whispers in his ear.

"Just one more drink and we can go back."

"My place or yours?"

"I'd like to see your place," says Emily, and the guilt that she has squashed so far grabs her heart as she thinks of her mother, alone in the house. She is glad that she hasn't told Ryan, the handsome stranger, because that is all that he is. Ryan signals to the bartender who comes over to take their orders.

"For the beautiful lady?" asks the bartender, winking at Emily.

"An old-fashioned for me," says Emily, averting her eyes and looking at Ryan.

"Whisky and soda," for me says Ryan and looks at the bartender directly in the eyes.

Emily sees the look and recognizes it with a mixture of regret because someone loved her once who didn't see her as a possession. She excuses herself from the bar to use the restroom and when she walks into the restroom she stands in front of the mirror and wonders what her father would have thought of her lifestyle if he had known. It was easy to hide secrets from him because he was busy at work and always seemed distracted. She was never able to hide secrets from her mother mainly because Molly was accepting of the choices that she had made even if she didn't fully understand them. She peers at her face, noting the carefully applied eyeliner and mascara and she thinks of the way in which Ryan looked at her and touched her body. She walks back into the bar, ready to go back to his place when she glances at a table and realizes that her client is sitting there with a woman. The woman is not his wife. She glances again and realizes it is a new romance. The woman is looking at her client with the eagerness of a young lover. Quickly, she walks back to the bar and tells Ryan that she wants to leave.

"What about your old-fashioned?"

"I've had enough to drink," says Emily.

They walk out of the bar and Ryan whispers in her ear again.

"Do you still want to come to my place?"

"Yes. I still want to come," says Emily, thinking about her client and realizing that his good looks and charm are a cover for something else.

She continues to talk to Ryan as they walk towards his car that is parked in one of the spots in the Historic Third Ward.

"I'm sorry we had to leave early," says Emily, "I saw my client in the bar, so I had to leave. It's not good practice to acknowledge clients outside the practice."

"Conflict of interest, I'm guessing."

Emily doesn't say a word and slips her hand into Ryan's because she feels a stab in her heart because of her father. Thinking about the client is a useful distraction although she has an uneasy feeling that she has been fooled by a charlatan. She thinks back to the first session with the client who told her that his wife wanted a divorce, and he still loved her, but he was willing to settle because he could see that she didn't love him anymore.

She thinks back to the first impressions and the way that he had smoothed his hair when Emily had walked into the room, but she had dismissed it as a sign of nervousness. Because the couple lived in Wisconsin, the law said that the property should be divided in half, but the client had shown her the agreement that he had drawn up and that his wife had agreed to. It left him with the bulk of the money because he had been the breadwinner. His wife had obtained a good settlement from the agreement and had a well-paid job, so it had seemed beneficial for both. For someone who was so distressed at losing his wife, Emily's client seemed quite content with the woman in the bar. The whole affair makes Emily very uncomfortable and now she is going home with a man, whom she barely knows, and she wonders what her father would have thought at all the strangeness in her life. She looks at Ryan again and there is something about him that makes her feel comfortable even if he is also a charlatan; she has had her share of questionable encounters. When they arrive at his apartment in lower east side of Milwaukee, she allows him to take off her clothes and he touches her in the most intimate of ways. She wakes up early in the morning and looks at him again, but there is little to feel, and she is numb. She slips out of the bed, writes a note, and leaves it on the dining room table. She has learned how to be quiet in the early hours of the morning. She creeps out of the apartment, phones for a cab, waits, and gets back to her apartment with a mixture of emotions. She smiles again at the second encounter with Ryan while feeling a pain in her stomach that refuses to go away. Her father has gone, and the reality of his death is hitting her. Sarah's evening at home after the loss of her father was more subdued. She had managed to reach her husband who was working nights at the hospital, just like her father had done for so many years.

"I'll try to leave early," Sam had said and, rather than protest, Sarah had thanked him for being considerate because the situation wasn't his fault. The situation had nothing to do with the loss of her father and everything to do with her or so she thought. Because in Sarah's mind, she had made a terrible mistake, and she blamed herself for what had happened. It had started a month ago when everything was going well at work and management had started to hire again after the pandemic had shred unnecessary personnel.

Being a research scientist for a prestigious pharmaceuticals company allowed Sarah to enjoy an enviable salary and job security. Although the incident happened only a month ago, it seems like a lifetime. It also went against her morals, because in all her relationships, Sarah had always been loyal, particularly to her husband and now she was smitten with someone else. Maybe it was something about his smile or the way that he looked at her. Or maybe it was his intellectual gaze that had attracted more than a second glance. All that Sarah knows is that she fell for Ian, and he fell for her. After his hire, Sarah and Ian had paired on a team project with two seniors looking forward to retirement. The pair had been enthusiastic about the project and had spent late nights together pouring over the data and analyzing the results from preliminary tests. It had seemed like a cliché to Sarah, yet she liked living the fantasy. The conversation had been formal and scientific yet there was something about the way that he looked at her and the way that he said things. Sarah had looked at his face a little more.

"We are replicating the results," Ian had said.

"And the magnitude is large. Almost 20 percent in variance," Sarah had said.

Because her husband was a doctor and focused on the practical side of science, Sarah had never shared with him the excitement of publishing in journals or detecting interactions within a complex analysis. She had chosen not to say anything after she realized that he never had the same level of excitement. When Ian came along, it was a different story. Sarah had fallen for someone like her. Now, she is unsure what to do and her father is dead. Her father has gone.

Four

Father Tom arrives at Molly's house as the clock strikes precisely three o'clock. Molly opens the door to welcome him, and she looks at his somber face, prepared for funeral arrangements. They walk into the living room together and Molly detects the scent of whisky on his breath but doesn't say a word because she is familiar with the catholic life even if Michael had lapsed in his attendance to the church. He was born a catholic and Molly respects the heritage even if she doesn't agree with all the rules. There are so many rules, yet they seem irrelevant in the face of a death.

"I am very sorry for your loss," says Father Tom, and Molly feels the warmth in his company. He might be a drinker, but his heart is in the right place. She remembers his kindness from earlier encounters when they had gone to church as a family, when her daughters were young and impressionable. Father Tom explains what will happen and assures Molly that she doesn't need to do anything. It is all taken care of.

"We have a very pleasant room in the basement for eating after the wake," says Father Tom, "I gather that Michael was an only child?"

"Yes, his parents died a few years ago. They were very proud of him. We have two daughters. I don't know if you remember them."

"Of course. They were pretty girls."

"Now they are beautiful women. They've done well in their professions. Emily is a lawyer."

Molly stands up and walks over to the table holding all the family photographs. She selects a picture of Michael with his two daughters.

"I took this photograph at Sarah's graduation. She is a scientist."

"He must have been very proud," says Father Tom.

"He was," says Molly, thinking of all their achievements. They had all been highflyers, including herself. Publication after publication and Molly had successfully treated many clients. Although retired, she still has her practice and the start of a novel – a murder mystery. Now her husband has gone, and retirement seems like a dream. She looks at the photograph of Michael again and wonders how she is going to manage.

Father Tom looks at Molly, remembering her from when she was younger.

"It must have been quite a shock for you. So sudden."

"It was an awful thing."

"Were there any signs?"

Molly shakes her head.

"He just had a full physical. He knew he needed to lose some pounds, but his specialist wasn't overly concerned. That's what he told me."

"You are always welcome back to the church Molly. It might help you."

"It's been so long. I might come. You know I wasn't catholic. I just joined Michael occasionally."

"You are still welcome. You are not a stranger."

Father Tom talks to Molly about the funeral and Molly starts to focus again, and his soothing words help her. At the same time, she feels a tightness around her throat, recalling all the occasions that she spent with Michael. She pushes away thoughts of the times when she thought of leaving him. Right now, it seems like a terrible nightmare. The reality of the moment is hitting her, and any thoughts of his failings are far away from her mind. The voice that has tormented her is taking a rest.

 The funeral arrives quickly on Friday morning with the service at 11am giving people enough time to drive from the Milwaukee suburbs into the downtown area of Juneau Town, one of the most popular areas of Milwaukee. The car arrives to take Molly, Emily, and Sarah to Michael's funeral. By now, Molly is outwardly calm, having gone to view Michael's body at the funeral home. There had been no visitation for friends. It had just been an occasion for Molly to visit him and her daughters had declined the invitation to view the body. She had touched his cheek and admired the work that the embalmer had done to make him presentable. In that moment, she had felt love for her husband despite the numbness in her hands.

The drive from the East Side to Juneau Town seems long to Molly and she feels her hands clench when she looks at the coffin in front of her. The funeral car is designed so that the coffin is found directly behind the driver and seats for family members are found at the back of the car. Molly tries to avert her eyes, but she keeps glancing at the wooden casket, trying to push away the memory of how he died. She glances at her daughters, but they are distracted. Sarah is frantically texting someone, and Molly is curious because she doesn't think it is Sam and she is itching to know. Emily is scrolling through social media posts, with a dazed expression on her face. Each of the women is engaging in trivial distractions so they don't have to focus on what has happened. The reality of Michael's death.

"We are here," says Molly when they arrive at the church. Everything looks strange and unreal, even the solidness of the church building. Molly gets out of the car and her daughters rush to her side, startled out of their distractions by the sudden arrival. They tuck their cellphones into their bags and walk with their mother into St. Mary's.

Molly looks at the statue of Mary as they walk inside, looking for some sign in the maelstrom. But she feels nothing and recognizes her numbness comes from shock and disbelief. Molly is relieved when Father Tom appears at the door to greet her and her daughters. She has forgotten all the details that he told her, and she watches as he sprinkles water onto the casket. There are few gatherers for Michael's funeral because he had no family but there are people that Molly recognizes from the hospital, some of whom she has known for many years, although not on a personal level. They smile at her with eyes of sadness as she walks down the aisle, and it all seems surreal, like a nightmare that is about to end. Still in a daze, she listens to Father Tom ask everyone to pray, and she closes her eyes. She closes her eyes again when Sarah reads a passage from the Bible, and she closes her eyes again when Emily reads a second passage. She blinks and opens up her eyes when it is all over and Sarah touches her arm to make sure that she is feeling fine, and all she wants to do is go home and sleep for a year, if not longer. Yet now there is food to be consumed in the large hall underneath the main church and Molly and her daughters walk down with Father Tom; the staff have laid out plates filled with sandwiches, quiches, and small delicacies to comfort the attendants. Molly slowly nibbles on a sandwich filled with ham and cheese and sips the glass of red wine that Father Tom has thrust into her hand.

"It will help you," he whispers in her ear, and she finds comfort in his presence. It is only when she spots Jay, one of Michael's colleagues, moving towards her that Molly tenses because she knows that Michael was close to him. They played golf together every week. Jay is an attractive man and Molly always got the impression that he was attracted to her. There had been a party where she had worn a fetching dress and Jay had whispered in her ear, "Michael is a very lucky man." His comment had belonged in a terrible romance novel and Molly had smiled and quickly moved away, slightly shocked by his audacity. She isn't surprised to see him at the funeral because he had enjoyed a friendship with Michael, so it is only fitting that he comes to pay his respects. Jay approaches her and touches her arm, and she is relieved that it is not a suggestive gesture.

"I am very sorry," he says, in the tone of voice suitable for a catholic funeral.

Molly thanks him for coming.

"I knew you and Michael were close," she says.

"Is there anything you need?"

Molly shakes her head, not wanting to convey an intimacy that is not there.

"Did something happen? I heard that he was running."

"He wanted to run again," says Molly, evading the truth yet she can see the puzzled look in Jay's eyes and knows that he wants more details. She is glad when Sarah, her daughter, comes over to bring more food.

"What time is the burial, Mom?" asks Sarah, handing Molly a plate of sandwiches.

"It's at 2pm. I can drive us down."

"You don't need to do that. I can drive," says Sarah.

Molly looks at her watch and realizes that there are a few

hours before the burial. All of Michael's friends have gathered in a circle and she plucks up courage and walks over to them to thank them for coming. There are no women in the circle, only men, and Molly overhears their conversation as she approaches.

"He was so devoted to the patients," says one of the senior physicians.

The senior physician turns around when he sees that Molly has joined the group and realizes his faux pas.

"And devoted to you."

"You are kind," says Molly, and feels a blush in her cheeks.

The conversation continues and Molly listens to the gentle banter swirling around the all-male group. She is daydreaming when one of the younger physicians speaks to her.

"What will you do with the house Dr. Williams?"

"Feel free to call me Molly. Everyone does."

She realizes that she hasn't even thought about the house. It is a large four bedroom with a den that was converted into a guest bedroom.

"We've lived in it for so many years. I don't really know. It's not something I've thought about."

She is glad when Emily joins her and tells her that she needs to leave.

"One of my clients texted me. It's an emergency. I need to review an agreement."

"Are you coming to the burial?" asks Molly.

"Of course. I'll meet you and Sarah down there."

Emily walks out of the hall and Molly feels alone and afraid. Feeling tired, Molly looks at her watch again and pushes away the need for a short nap. She glances at her daughter Sarah, who is talking to Father Tom.

The look of strain in Sarah's eyes is lifting and Molly wonders what is on Sarah's mind. She wishes she could switch off her trained clinician eyes, but she finds it difficult when it is her daughter. The shadows under Sarah's eyes tell Molly that she is sleep deprived and even an untrained acquaintance would be able to spot the neglect in sleep. She does not catch Sarah's attention so walks over to her and tells her that she wants to go home for a rest.

"Of course, mom. Let's just leave. I'm tired too."

"We can both have a nap back at the house," says Molly, "before we go to the cemetery."

The pair tell Father Tom that they will see him later and they walk out of the room, glad to be out of the swirl of the crowd. Sarah drives back to the house saying little to her mother because her mind is also in a daze. It is the weekend, and she normally finds some time to see Ian because of Sam's shifts at the hospital.

She feels selfish for wanting to see him and guilty for feeling the desire to be with him. Molly slides out of her dress and puts on her robe. She curls onto the bed, looking at the vastness of the room and she thinks again about what she wants to do with the house. Should she stay or should she leave?

Her mind races with thoughts, many of them illogical and her head spins. Eventually, Molly closes her eyes and falls into a deep sleep. An hour later, the alarm wakes her out of the slumber. She looks at the clock and realizes that they need to get ready to go to the cemetery. She hears movement downstairs and gets out of the bed. She feels a chill in the air as she puts on clothing suitable for an outside burial. Molly walks down the stairs to find Sarah fully dressed and texting furiously.

"Is everything fine?" asks Molly

"Just a friend," says Sarah, quickly shutting her cellphone. Mother and daughter walk out of the house and feel the brisk Wisconsin wind in their faces. It is April and while Wisconsinites hope for an early summer, spring can turn from delight into unpleasantness in a single moment. And Molly wonders if it is just her imagination, but she feels a coldness in her bones that reminds her of stark winters in England when her parents tried to keep the house warm.

Curled up in front of a coal fire, Molly had savored the bread and strawberry jam that her mother had given her. It was a favorite treat for most English school children. The coldness of the change in temperatures reminds her of a time when life had been carefree. She looks at her daughter who is driving and wonders how they will get through this. The cemetery is just north of Milwaukee in the county of Ozaukee and Sarah is using her phone to find the place. Molly looks out of the window as the scenery turns from urban skyrises to rolling hills along the lakefront. They arrive at the cemetery and Sarah parks the car. Both women stretch, still sleepy from the afternoon nap and they get out of the car and watch Emily pull up in her own car, not far behind them. Molly sighs with relief because she is always unsure whether Emily is going to show to family events, although today is an exceptional event. Emily was never close to her father, so Molly is appreciative of Emily's presence at the funeral. Michael was closer to Sarah because he had never understood his youngest daughter's casual love life.

"I'm glad you are here," says Molly, touching Emily's arm.

"I rushed to get here," says Emily, "The client was frustrating."

"I'm sure," says Molly and the three women walk down the path towards the grave. Molly is relieved to see Father Tom standing by the graveside. It is a short service and Molly watches Father Tom sprinkle dirt onto the coffin, and she remembers the times that they have spent as family. It is not clear to her how things will unfold yet she has always had an instinct for when changes are coming. Again, she thinks back to the home that they have owned for the last two decades, and she is starting to appreciate the suggestion by the young physician. It is time to move and find a smaller place for herself. The house was designed for a family. Their children moved and started their own lives. It is time for Molly to do the same.

Five

A few days after the funeral, it is midnight. Molly is wide awake and is itching to get out of bed and to do something, but she is unsure what to do. Tomorrow, she is meeting with the estate lawyer to discuss the provisions within Michael's will.

It is not the meeting that concerns her but knowing that Michael left the bulk of his estate to her; in the case of her death, Emily and Sarah would receive the inheritance with Sam, Sarah's husband, a close third. She thinks about Sam for a moment because he didn't come to the funeral and Sarah has been evasive about the reasons why, citing work commitments and shortage of staff, amid the pandemic. Molly looks at the clock again and finding sleep impossible, she gets out of bed and walks downstairs to the living room, spotting the laptop on the coffee table. It has been over a week since she has worked on the first draft of the novel, and she feels a sudden desire to finish the book, so it is ready for the editor. She can't belief that a top publishing company has provided her with a contract for her first book. She knows it is an exception rather the rule and she is excited that her murder mystery novel will be distributed globally. She carries the laptop up to the bedroom and opens the machine, finding the manuscript safely stored on the hard drive. She smiles as she finds the place where she finished the last edit and reads the description of her detective, tall, dark, and handsome with a host of maladies and irritations as befits an English detective. She combs the text, finding comfort in the minor editing of punctuation and grammar problems. The developmental editor has helped with the plot and storyline and all that is needed is for the proofreader to correct the manuscript after Molly's final effort. After thirty minutes, her eyes droop and Molly feels sleep beckoning her back to a place between the sheets. She shuts the laptop and gathers the sheets around her, feeling the warmth from the blanket to cover her body. Because she is slender, she always feels cold. Sleep grabs her back and when Molly falls asleep, there are no messy dreams of Michael, running and crashing. It is the deepest sleep she has had in the week. When she wakes up in the morning, she feels more refreshed, yet she knows that she is in trouble. Any desire to move from the bed evades her so she stretches her arms behind her and allows her fingers to touch the headstand. The movement stirs her, and she thinks of hot tea. The image is enough to force her out of bed and she walks to the wardrobe and slips into a dressing gown to keep her warm. She walks down the stairs, clutching the laptop to her chest, like a mother holding a newborn. All her movements are on autopilot; she feels like a robot. Molly is dissociating, moving from fight to flight to freeze without knowing.

"What am I doing?" she says out loud and the sound of her

voice wakes her up. She is alone in the house and Michael is gone. After she makes the tea, she walks into the living room and picks up her cellphone, wondering why she hasn't spoken to her therapist in so long. She feels the need.

"Patty. I need to see you," says Molly, "Michael has died."

"I'm so sorry to hear this. I can see you today. I have an opening at 1pm," says Patty," It will be good to see you. It's been a while."

"I've missed you," says Molly.

Patty Brown's office is in Juneau Town and is a short drive from Molly's house. Molly slips out of the house and gets in the car, wondering what she is going to say to Patty after several years away. A flurry of words and short speeches swirl in her mind and she mentally rehearses the carefully chosen words, knowing they will end up on the cutting room floor. Molly's foot presses on the accelerator and she tries to slow herself down, trying to relief her anxiety. It's been a long time since she has seen her therapist.

Patty helped her when her father died and, after healing, she felt a bond with her, particularly as they are both clinicians. She walks into the small clinic, wearing her mask and tells the receptionist that she has come to see Patty. Molly sits down on the couch in the reception area and waits. The five-minute wait seems intolerable, and she is relieved when Patty flutters into the area, smiles, and gestures to Molly to enter the sanctuary of the therapist's office. Molly sits on the chair close to the door, looks at Patty's face and feels relaxed. A select few can create such ease. Without the formal introductions that normally take place between a therapist and client, Molly launches into a recount of what happened the day that Michael collapsed, not missing any of the details. Molly smiles when Patty asks the most tried and tested therapist question.

"How did you feel?"

"It was terrible. I realized he was having an episode. I was in shock when he had the attack."

"How do you feel now?"

"Right now, I feel a mixture of anger, sadness, and regret."

"Regret? What does that look like for you?"

"That's a good question. I've thought about our marriage this week. Surprisingly, I've accepted he's gone. It's been surreal. You see I feel that he was gone long before he died."

Molly looks at Patty for a moment, feeling the same sense of ease that she experienced when she went to the weekly sessions. Patty is an expert in grief on relationships and death and she has met all kinds of situations. Some people never stop grieving a loss and some are glad that it happened. Patty senses the tension within Molly and is reminded that she was one of her favorite clients, when she used to come. Now, she is back, and things have changed. Molly continues to talk about the loss and as she does so, the tension inside eases because she is starting to heal.

"I never told you this," says Molly, "I thought of leaving him a few years ago. It was before my dad died. I just didn't think it was relevant."

"It was relevant to you then," says Patty.

"I met someone. There was no affair. It was at a conference. One of the yearly academic conferences that I attend. He was from England."

"Just like you," says Patty with a smile.

"It was really a brief encounter. It was the first time in years that a man made me feel desirable. He told me that I was very attractive."

"You met a man who made you feel good," says Patty.

Molly hangs her head, and she feels embarrassed for sharing about the incident. Patty looks at Molly seeing a very beautiful woman in her sixties. A woman whom other women admire because of her light hair, soft complexion, and slim figure from exercise and healthy eating.

"Everyone needs love," says Patty, "Even you."

"I know. I felt so guilty about it. I'm always trying to become more self-aware and tap into my emotions. But sometimes, it feels hazy."

"You are in shock over Michael's death."

"It was unexpected. As a therapist, I know what to do yet I feel stuck. It seems ridiculous. Michael left everything to me and I'm financially stable, but I don't like being in the house."

"I'm sure there are so many memories. Have you considered selling and moving to a new place?"

"Really, that would be the best choice. I've lived there so long and I'm feeling a pull away from the place. I plan to get in touch with a realtor and put the house on the market. Funny enough, the one place I really want to be right now is England. Just visit London or somewhere good along the south coast."

Molly's eyes fill with tears, and she looks around Patty's office for tissues. The box is placed on the coffee table yet is not at arm's reach, so Molly jumps out of the sofa and grabs it. The tears pour down her face and she wipes her face dry. She shakes her head and looks at Patty.

"It always helps to cry. I've been holding it all in Patty. I'm so English at times." Molly throws the tissue in the wastepaper basket and smiles at Patty, feeling the release of emotion. They talk some more and once her face is dry, Molly stands up and thanks Polly.

"Will you come back and see me?" asks Patty.

"You know I will," says Molly.

Patty presses a card into Molly's hand.

"This young woman is very good. She is trained in all the new techniques. I've heard that miracles happen with brainspotting. She's a consultant."

Molly looks at the card and thinks about all the ways in which trauma leaves a mark on the body. Some choose to eat their way through misery, and she chooses to run.

"I do know about it," she says, "I'll think about it."

She touches Patty's arm and leaves the office feeling a great sense of relief. Molly drives home feeling the warmth in her body and is reminded of the luxury of being a client, rather than a therapist. A sense of normalcy returns to her mind that was troubled by the past and all the memories of Michael. Despite his limitations, she loved him yet somewhere in the marriage they drifted apart, and he became a stranger to her. She tries to remember the last time he made love to her and realizes it was several years before he died. His weight gain and long hours at the hospital had diminished his desire to be with her and she had lost interest too.

She intends to drive home yet her sense of release prompts her to drive a little further into the lower east side so she can have a cup of coffee. The thought of a cappuccino appeals to her. She realizes that she has plenty of time on her hands now that her college job is over. It is a Thursday, and the coffee shop is half full because most of the clients come in the early morning before the journey to work. She sits at the table and eats the foam that has formed on the top of the coffee. She licks the foam from her mouth, feeling like an English school girl again. She glances up and watches a tall and handsome man wearing glasses walk into the coffee store. He is looking at his phone and he doesn't see Molly, but she sees him. She smiles in delight when she realizes that she is looking at her fictional detective. This is exactly how she imagined him. He is not classically handsome but there is something appealing in the way his glasses sit on the tip of his nose. Realizing that she is looking too hard, she looks away and when she looks up, she notices him looking at her. His gaze is subtle and not crude. Just an appreciation of a beautiful woman. She sips from her coffee again and looks out of the window. When she looks again, he has left the café and for a moment she feels disappointed that he is no longer in the place. She finishes her coffee and drives home, thinking about the novel again. She wants to read through it so she can work on the description of her detective. The detective who looks good in circular glasses and has a mystery to solve. Molly also realizes that she needs to write some sequels because the detective is someone who deserves to be with someone. When she thinks back to the man whom she saw in the café, it strikes her that there was no ring on his finger, yet she guesses that he is with someone. He is too attractive to be a single man. Molly goes home, pours water into the electric kettle, gazes out of the window and sings an English ballad. It is a love song, and she thinks back to the men whom she has known and of her husband, whom she didn't really know, even though she used to think that she did. Molly sits on the sofa and is sipping her tea when the phone rings. It is Sarah, her daughter.

"How are you mom? I'm checking in."

"I'm better. I went for coffee and now I'm back home."

"Did you see the therapist?"

"It was good to see her. She was very helpful."

"I'm thinking I might go and see her. I still have the card you gave me."

"You were so close to your dad."

The women talk a little longer with Molly detecting that Michael's death won't be the only thing that Sarah will discuss with Patty. Quite often a death is a time for reflection on relationships that are dying. She walks back into the kitchen and pours herself another cup of tea. She thinks about Emily, her younger daughter, and the struggles that she is facing in her job as a lawyer. But Emily is thinking of other things. Tomorrow is court day for her client, and she doesn't want to be there because she knows that he is a liar, and it is making her uncomfortable. When her cellphone rings and Emily sees that it is Ryan, she hesitates for a moment because she needs to go to bed early and be ready for court. Emily is direct and to the point, keeping her tone professional without a trace of romance.

"I'm in court tomorrow."

"But I want to see you."

"I can't go out."

"I'll come over. I'll pick up some sushi."

"That works," says Emily, thinking of Ryan in bed with her.

A sliver of guilt and pleasure seeps into her body and she touches the folds, contemplating the possibility of going on a diet, even though she knows that Ryan doesn't really care. It is a typical evening with Ryan. Light chatters over food before descending into the depths of the sheets. It is only when Ryan touches her that she finds different feelings invading her mind. The usual tingle of excitement and pleasure and pangs of guilt, which is unusual for Emily because she has not had those feelings in a while. The guilt is enough for her to feel human and after it is over, she touches his arm feeling some remorse that she doesn't care for him in the way that other women would care. Ryan is a good-looking man, a cool man her friends would say. She takes her hand away from him and turns towards the wall, waiting for sleep to catch up with her. It is still early, and sleep comes quickly after the intimacy. Emily dreams and she is swimming in a lagoon in some far-away place with a man, who is not Ryan. A man whom she hasn't thought of in a long time and now he is back in her arms in a far-away dream utopia.

Six

Emily is still in bed with Ryan, and it is court day for her client. She manages to get herself out of bed, puts on a robe, and walks into the kitchen to make coffee. After pouring the water into the French press, she waits for the coffee, feeling impatient because she wants to get dressed. Once it is ready, she walks back into the bedroom clutching two mugs. Ryan is awake and sitting up in bed and, for a moment, she imagines being with him for a long day between the sheets, until she remembers the court case.

"I need to get ready," says Emily.

"Later tonight?" asks Ryan.

Emily doesn't say anything.

"I'll take you out tonight," says Ryan, "after your case."

"I need a rest," says Emily, "Go out with your friends."

"You can come with us," says Ryan.

Emily shakes her head, tired of all the banter. Instead, she peers into the wardrobe, carefully selecting a blouse and skirt that is right for the court room. After pulling on the cream blouse and plaid skirt, she walks into the bathroom and washes her face with water, before applying eyeshadow to her lids. She applies the rest of her make-up, thinking of the night with Ryan and contemplating the moves and shifts of the evening. She smiles as she applies lipstick and looks in the mirror, deciding not to apply rouge or foundation. She looks in the mirror again and thinks of her father because she looks like him. She inherited his dark looks and Sarah is fair, just like Molly. She feels a stiffness in her neck and massages the area with her hand, before walking back into the bedroom. Ryan is dressed and is sitting on the bed, smiling at her.

"Do you still like me, Emily?" asks Ryan

"You know I do," she says, "but I need to go."

They leave the condo together and Ryan walks across the road to his car. Emily watches him again, feeling the desire inside her body. Because Ryan is a good-looking man, and she has always enjoyed the kick of being with someone who is handsome. A few hours later, she is in the courthouse with her client, who is smoothing his hair and looking at the judge, who is a woman presiding over the case. The hearing is brief because Emily has prepared the case well. In the State of Wisconsin, divorce law stipulates that property is divided equally. The judge does not consider emotional elements in the case such as the whys of the disintegration. It is purely based on property built over the length of the relationship. Emily thinks back to the first time that she met with the client. He had shown Emily the agreement that his wife had signed granting him sixty percent of the estate. The client had given no reason for this inequity in distribution apart from saying, "she signed the form," before handing it to Emily, his lawyer.

The client is sitting beside Emily in the courthouse and his hand is, once again, straightening his hair. The client has always won, particularly with women who consider him good-looking, but Emily can now see through the façade. It's a skill that she learned from her mother even if it came a little too late with this client. The judge reads the agreement that Emily has handed to her. She stamps the papers and declares the decree nisi valid. Emily looks at her client: he has a look of smugness on his face happens when the plaintiff has won a large assessment. In the case of her client, it is not the money that appears to be the reward: it is the fact that he has won that pleases him. Emily shifts in her chair and feels uncomfortable so is glad when the client shakes her hand and quickly leaves the courthouse. Emily wonders which one of his women he is meeting and how long he got away with deceiving his wife. She smiles at the judge, closes her bag, and heads out of the courthouse, relieved that she won't see the client again. She looks at her watch, and it is four o'clock. After settling the case for her client, Emily feels the need for a martini to celebrate the win. If it could be called a win. She drives her car down into the Third Ward Area and finds a parking spot close to the Journeyman Hotel. The hotel is quiet in the afternoon, and she takes the elevator to the roof top. She spots the man in the cowboy hat straightaway because she knows that he is checking her out. She orders her drink, and it isn't long before he comes over.

"I'm not going to hit on you," he says, "Here's my card. If you ever want to go out sometime."

Emily smiles and tucks the card into her wallet. Without saying a word, she drowns the rest of the martini, gets out of the seat and leaves the hotel, glad that she didn't have to wear a mask because she is fully vaccinated. She gets back to her car and wonders when it will all end. The pandemic and the fling with Ryan. Handsome, superficial Ryan who likes to eat sushi and hang out with his friends. She gets home, boils a pan of water, and tosses the spaghetti into the pan. Once the food is ready, she pours the spaghetti into a bowl and pours herself a glass of red wine. She drinks it quickly, thinking about her day and how she feels about the client. He was an older man, a little younger than her dad and she can't help but compare the two. Her father was distant with her and slightly dull whereas the client was Casanova. Emily has met several Casanovas in her job as a family lawyer yet there is something very unsettling about the latest client and she tries to think what it is that is bothering her. He is handsome, clean cut, athletic, intelligent, and cultured. Emily takes another sip of wine, and thinks about the puzzle of her client, why she feels uncomfortable, and she wishes that her mother was with her right now because she would have the clinical insight. On impulse, she picks up the cellphone, takes another sip of wine and calls Molly.

"How was your court case?" asks Molly, who is quick to pick up the phone.

"It went well. The client got his settlement. I wanted to ask you about something that is bothering me. It's about the client."

"Did something about him bother you?" asks Molly.

"His wife agreed to a settlement, and he got sixty percent of the money. She signed it willingly. I saw him with another woman in a bar one night so I'm guessing he met someone else. It's just that there was something creepy about him. It made me doubt my first beliefs. He seemed so charming when we first met. Any thoughts?"

"Well," said Molly, "There are signs of narcissism. They do tend to be very charming when you first meet them. It's also superficial."

"There was something about his eyes too. Like he wasn't quite real."

"They do tend to wear a mask to hide their fragile ego," says Molly.

"Thanks. I did wonder."

"I can lend you my DSM 5 manual if you want to learn more. It will help if you have another client like him."

The conversation ends and Emily finishes the last drops of wine, places the glass in the sink, not wanting to wash it, and she yawns, feeling ready for sleep. She tucks herself into bed and banishes thoughts of the client through imagining herself in Mexico without a man, swimming in a lagoon with a multitude of fish. And she realizes why the client has disturbed her psyche. He reminds her of so many of the men that she dated. One-night stands, romances that blew up, and men who scared her. Emily looks back and it seems like a haze. A quick succession of men after a bad breakup from someone who didn't care for her. She feels the pain run through her body remembering the experience and feeling the torture that he is no longer in her life. She closes her eyes again and takes deep breaths knowing this is the first time she has considered all the men and the consequences of her actions. It has taken the death of her father to challenge her. To consider whether this is a journey she wants to continue to take. Despite the lack of closeness to her father, she loved him and knew that he cared about her choices. Her choices that were in opposition to her sister, who met and married the man of her dreams.

The following morning, Molly wakes up and thinks about the manuscript because it is ready for the editor. She thinks about her detective again and the man that she saw in the coffee shop. Feeling slightly reckless, she dresses and tucks the laptop into her bag. She pushes away the critic's voice in her head that tells her he won't be there, but the voice still lingers so she is surprised when she arrives at the place, and spots him straight away. The man is still handsome, looking like her imaginary detective. He is sitting at a table, looking at his phone with an expectant look on his face. She pays for her coffee, looking for a spare table, but the café is full of young people who are stuck at home because of the lack of in-person college classes. The man glances up at her, smiles, and calls out to her. He has a booming voice, and it is not what Molly expects. She imagined her detective to be soft-spoken.

"You can sit here," he says, gesturing towards the chair.

"Oh, thank you. You are kind."

Feeling slightly nervous about meeting him again, Molly quickly opens the laptop and finds the place where she finished editing. She looks up and the man is sipping his coffee. He is reading a book that looks familiar to Molly.

"Oh, Faulkner," she says, feeling herself blush because, up close, he is even more attractive.

"Trying to get through it again. I read it at college."

"It's the only one of his that I had read," says Molly.

"Did you like it?"

"I think so. I remember loving the language. I don't think I really understood it. I was too young."

The man looks at her again, appraising her quiet beauty.

"I'm Miles," he says and smiles.

"Molly from England."

Miles laughs and Molly feels a warm glow in her body, again noting that he isn't wearing a ring. She thinks of Michael and feels guilty.

"I have Scottish heritage," says Miles, "My last name is

McGowan."

"Have you been to Scotland?"

"To Edinburgh. When I was married. The driving was terrible."

"This is the problem with the British. They drive on the wrong side of the road."

Miles laughs again and Molly smiles because it is starting to feel like a date with the usual chit-chat that is fun and superficial. It is only when Miles looks at his watch and curses that the magic suddenly disappears.

"I'm late. I promised my fiancé that I would pick up some bread."

"It was good to meet you," says Molly, feeling a stab of disappointment. He is taken by another, and she is embarrassed, worried that he might have detected that she is attracted to him. She has seen far greater scenes of disappointment in her role as therapist, but it still stings. She watches him grab his bag and run out of the door, with a worried look on his face. She wonders about the character of the fiancée. A woman who insists that the man picks up bread. She returns to her manuscript and although she is not in the mood to continue editing, she attacks the manuscript with the precision of a professional editor. Half-way through, she gets another cup of coffee, and the minutes tick by as Molly gets into a flow, feeling compelled to finish the edit. She reaches the final page and smiles when she scans the document, noting the lack of red. She tucks the laptop back into her bag and returns home, calling her editor as soon as she gets back. "I'll send it to you right now," says Molly, firing up her laptop again and feeling the sense of accomplishment when her finger presses the send key.

"I've got it," says the editor.

Feeling a need for celebration early in the day, Molly has a sudden desire to lace up her running shoes and run fast through the streets of Upper East Side Milwaukee. She changes into her running clothes, puts on her watch, and heads out of the house, with headphones clipped over her ears. Music is booming. She starts slowly and after five minutes, the beat of the music encourages her to pick up the pace. She runs into Lake Park, admiring the lighthouse and lions along the way and then takes several laps around the park itself before heading towards Shorewood, the village of birds. Half-way through, Molly turns around and runs back towards Lake Park. She is about to cross the road that leads into the park when she sees Miles. She looks around expecting him to be with his fiancée, but he is alone, and she wonders if he picked up the bread in time for dinner. Miles is standing at the corner of Kenwood and Lake Drive. She waits for a moment to catch his attention until she realizes that he is struggling to catch his breath. Molly rushes over to help him, suddenly scared for his safety.

"I can't breathe," he says, and he grabs hold of Molly's arm.

Molly dips into her pocket and pulls out an inhaler.

"Try this," she says.

Miles places the inhaler in his mouth and takes two deep breaths. He lets go of Molly's arm and tries to recognize her. Despite the fog in his head, it comes to him. She is the attractive woman from the coffee shop.

"Feeling better?" asks Molly.

Miles takes another breath and nods, regaining his balance on the edge of the pavement.

"Thank you," he says.

"I'm glad you are feeling better," says Molly and places the inhaler back into her pocket.

"You run too?" asks Miles, realizing that Molly is dressed in running clothes and feeling normalcy return.

"It keeps me sane," says Molly, with a mischievous smile.

"I run too," says Miles, "although not very well."

Molly looks at him and watches the color return to his cheeks.

"Something terrible happened," says Miles.

"What is wrong?" asks Molly.

"Liv. It's over."

"Liv is your fiancé?" asks Molly.

Miles nods and Molly sees the anguish in his eyes.

"It just happened."

"You are in some shock," says Molly, realizing why he couldn't catch his breath. Miles looks at her and it seems to Molly that he doesn't recognize her. She reaches out to touch him and he looks at her, suddenly gaining focus again.

"I'm sorry," he says. "I lost it."

"No need to apologize. I see this quite often. You are in pain. Can I help you?"

"It's fine. I parked the car. I was afraid I'd have an accident. Can I take you somewhere?"

Molly shakes her head and points at her watch. Miles laughs at the humor.

"I used to be fast," he says.

"So did I," says Molly, "Until life slowed me down."

Miles thanks her again and she smiles, and he watches Molly run across the road, and into the park. It is a start.

Seven

It is a start to a new thing and when Molly walks into the coffee shop the following day, she is not surprised to see Miles sitting at the same table. He looks up when she walks in and Molly smiles at him. He gets out of his seat and walks over.

"Let me get you coffee," he says, and Molly thanks him.

She sits down at the table and watches Miles order the coffee, aware that something has happened between them. It is the feeling of intimacy that surprises Molly because although she finds him physically attractive, there is something else that draws her to him. He walks over with the coffee, and places it in front of her.

"Do you want any cream?" he asks, and Molly shakes her head, bowing her head slightly because when she looks at him, she feels shy.

"What are you thinking?" he asks and Molly smiles at him trying to find the right words to dispel the idea that there is something between them. Something intimate.

"I was thinking about England," says Molly, replying with a quick response because she doesn't want him to know what she was really thinking.

"Do you visit often?" he asks.

Molly shakes her head.

"It's been several years."

"Do you think of moving back?"

Molly laughs and shakes her head.

"My home is here. I have two daughters. They live in Milwaukee."

Miles smiles and looks at Molly's hand, noting there is no ring on her finger. He looks at her again and realizes that she is even more beautiful than he remembered when they first met in the café. It makes him feel good and afraid.

"I apologize for all of my questions," he says, "It's because I'm a lawyer."

"Litigation?"

"I'm on the poor end of the spectrum," says Miles.

"Surely not public defender."

"Estate planning," says Miles, "I work for the very wealthy."

Molly looks at him again, noting the kindness in his eyes.

"You must have helped a lot of families," she says.

"I try," he says and looks at her again noting the blueness in her eyes. Realizing that he has spoken about himself, he tries to find out more about her.

"What about you? Retired?"

"Yes and no," says Molly, with a laugh in her voice and Miles feels some semblance of normalcy enter his life.

"I retired from the university. I was a professor. I'm a clinician and still work with clients. I have a private practice. I just serve the wealthy, not the super-rich. Essentially, the middle-class."

"Therapy. One of life's luxuries," says Miles, looking at his watch.

"Do you need to be somewhere?" asks Molly.

"A work meeting but we can talk some more, if you like," he says, noting the curve of her lips, and wondering what it would feel like to kiss them.

They continue to talk, and Molly leans forward and feels the intimacy between them, aware that they have just experienced something traumatic because Miles is still upset and needs someone to talk to. It just happens to be her. She is lost in the moment and is startled when she looks up and sees Jay walking towards them. The last time she saw Jay was at Michael's funeral and she tenses because she remembered how he looked at her. She smiles at Jay, feeling like a mannequin because her smile feels like plastic.

"Hello Molly," says Jay, "how are you? It's good to see you."

Jay looks at Miles and smiles, waiting for an introduction.

"Good to see you too," says Molly, "I'm fine."

Jay stands in place, appraising the situation.

"This is Miles," says Molly, "A friend of mine."

The two men shake hands and Molly sees the discomfort in Miles' face, because Jay is full of punch and pride.

"Molly and I go back a long way," says Jay, with a smug expression on his face. Miles smiles politely and looks down at his coffee.

There is a silence that captures the three in an imaginary cage, and Molly stays quiet because Jay is eager for action and is not gaining from the situation. Jay smiles again and looks over at the counter, spotting the attractive barista who always serves him coffee.

"I need to go," he says, "Just came into grab some coffee."

After he leaves, Molly looks at Miles and smiles.

"A friend of yours?" he asks.

"Not really. He used to work with my husband."

"Oh," says Miles and a wave of disappointment sweeps across his face, "I didn't realize you were married. I am stupid. Of course, you have daughters."

Molly tenses again wanting to tell Miles everything yet scared of sharing. She tries to speak but the flashback arrives without warning. It is sudden and Molly's mind plays tricks on her. She blinks and is back at the graveyard, burying Michael. The priest is scattering the dirt on top of the coffin. She can't cry and she pinches her hand to get out of the memory. She is back in the coffee store and Miles is still drinking his coffee. 'The reality slams hard waking her up and she looks at Miles with a sense of urgency.

"He died," she says, finding herself repeating the words, "he died."

"He died?" says Miles, "I am sorry. I didn't know."

"I'm so tired", says Molly and she shakes her head in disbelief that she has been fooling herself because he really has gone, and she is sitting in a café with a man she barely knows. A man whom she has just met yet Miles seems like an old friend in that moment.

"I'm sorry," she says, "I don't want to play the victim. You are going through so much."

A haze crosses Mile's eyes. He recalls the moment when Liv told him that it was over, and it is only when Molly looks at him again that he realizes he has found someone to tell. The story of Liv, a woman whom he loved in such a frenetic moment that he lost himself in her.

"You are still in shock," says Molly and her hand reaches across the table to touch his fingers.

"I don't know where to start," says Miles, seeing the compassion in Molly's face.

"You have already started," says Molly, "You showed up today. That is something."

"Is it?" asks Miles and confusion sweeps into his mind as he considers how it ended.

"How did you meet?"

"It was nine months ago," says Miles, "I'm busy as an attorney. A friend suggested online dating."

"It can be quite successful," says Molly, "I know some people who met the one through an online site."

"Well, I thought she was the one."

"I'm sure you did," says Molly.

"Was your husband the one?" asks Miles.

Molly pauses for a moment and considers the question because it's been so long since she thought about it.

"For a long time," she says.

"Have you been widowed long?"

Molly takes a sharp intake of breath as she thinks about all that has happened during the last few weeks: the retirement party, the trip to Indiana, the episode, the run, the ambulance, and the burial. The events move quickly through her memory like a film reel with Molly acting as a detached observer. She grips her hand and is back in reality, taking in the cup of coffee and Miles sitting across from her.

"Did you hear me?" asks Miles and Molly shakes her head.

"Sorry, I just lost it," she says, smiling at Miles as is her custom, and asking him to repeat the question.

"It was two weeks ago," she says, thinking of the strangeness of linear time.

"I had no idea," says Miles, "You have been through something."

"We are still in shock, but we are doing well. My daughters are quite hardy. They flew the nest a long time ago."

"And here am I," says Miles, "Deep in my shock and I don't know what to say to you."

"As I said, you don't need to say a word."

They finish their coffee and get out of their seats, and Miles walks towards Molly with a look of intent.

"I forgot to thank you for the other day. When we met in Lake

Park."

"It was a good coincidence," says Molly, looking at his face and wondering why he seems so familiar and thinking to herself that he has a good face. The kind of face to come home to every evening. The guilt returns because they are both free. Miles is not engaged anymore, and Michael has gone.

She feels like a child in the playground, irresponsible, and without knowledge of the rules of moral society. In this moment of infancy, she walks towards the door with a sudden urge to see Miles again.

They walk out into the sunshine and Molly looks up at the sky, basking in the warmth. Miles seems so close although there is physical distance between the two. It is only when she looks down the street that she feels a sense of fear, and a chill of insecurity seeps into her body and she freezes. Because there, on the corner, is someone who looks like Sarah, her daughter, and she can't believe it is her because she is kissing someone, and it isn't Sam. It is not Sarah's husband. It is not the kiss of friendship, but a kiss exchanged by lovers. Molly wants to rush towards the woman to stop her, but she isn't sure if it is Sarah, so she stays and turns towards Miles, and she kisses him with the passion of a teenage lover.

"I'm so sorry," she says, after the kiss and she looks into Miles' eyes and sees a look of bewilderment. Miles is dazed and he doesn't see Molly. In his mind, he is looking into the eyes of Liv, his former fiancée, a woman who has rejected him. He is in a trance. Molly spots a bench across the road from the coffee shop, and she walks him across the road, constantly aware that he is detached from the situation. They sit on the bench next to each other and Molly looks at him again, gradually watching him return to normality.

"I don't know what came over me. Kissing you like that," she says with a pink blush on her cheeks.

"You don't need to apologize to me," says Miles, "I enjoyed it."

Miles' eyes glisten like drops on a blanket of rich soil.

"Your eyes are very brown," she says.

"You are very pretty," says Miles and she blushes again at the sudden intimacy.

"Do you want to talk about it?" asks Molly.

"Talk about what?" asks Miles

"About what happened. Between you and your fiancée."

"Oh. You mean Liv? My ex."

"Like a therapist and client?" asks Miles and Molly laughs.

"You have an English sense of humor," she says.

Because the weather is calm for Wisconsin, they choose to walk down towards the lakefront and they watch the waves, some billowing, some clambering for attention from the shoreline. As they walk and talk, the story of Miles and Liv emerges.

"At the beginning, it was perfect," says Miles, "she told me that I had saved her from loneliness."

"How did she help you?"

"I had been lonely too," says Miles, "I'd been alone for a decade after the divorce. I didn't meet anyone. I just worked and saw my son at the weekends. After my son left the area, it became very hard."

They walk towards Veteran's Park and look at the birds flying across the pond slowly making their way back to the mid-west after the chill of winter. Molly looks at Miles again and sees the anguish in his face as he recalls the nine months that he spent with Liv.

"I was married for over twenty years," says Miles, "but this break-up is hurting more than the divorce."

"It seems that it was unexpected," says Molly.

"The day we spoke, I went to Liv's place, and she was waiting for me at the front door. All my belongings were in the hallway. She had packed everything. She said that she didn't like the dynamic between us."

"Didn't like the dynamic? That's a strange thing to say."

"I blame myself," says Miles, "I'm not the easiest of people."

"You seem fine to me," said Molly, "I meet all sorts of people in my line of work."

"So do I," says Miles and they look at each other and laugh.

"I appreciate that not all lawyers are snakes," says Molly.

"I try to be decent," says Miles.

"I went to a clinicians' conference a few years ago. There was a symposium on psychopaths in the workplace," says Molly.

"Really? I didn't realize they worked."

Molly laughs again, delighting in the play between them.

"Yes, they aren't all serial killers. Many are quite successful because they ingratiate themselves with senior management. They can be charming."

Molly looks at Miles and notices a puzzled look on Miles' face.

"It's strange," he says, "But even though Liv and I were getting married, I'm not sure that I really knew her."

"She obviously meant a lot to you," says Molly, "be glad for that. Even if it ended badly, there is a lesson in these kinds of experiences. I'm finding this out myself."

"Yes, that was a shock for you. A sudden death. Worse than my own. My situation seems trivial compared to yours."

"It was bad. It still is. I can't deny it. It normally takes a year to heal from a loss. My daughters are very supportive of me."

"What was his name?"

"Michael. He was a doctor. A busy man."

"That sounds like me. The client always comes first," says Miles, looking at his phone. They stop walking for a moment and Miles responds to a text message.

"Was that one of your clients?" asks Molly after he finishes the message.

"I need to draw up an agreement," says Miles, looking at his watch. He looks at Molly and feels a flicker of sadness because he has enjoyed spending time with her.

"Do you want to meet again?" he asks.

"I'd enjoy it," says Molly and she reaches into her bag and

takes out her business card. On the back, she writes down her personal phone number.

"I'll call you soon," says Miles, and in a moment, he is gone, returning to his car and his job as a busy lawyer. He drives to the office in a daze, thinking about the week's events yet mindful that he is driving and that he almost had a car accident after Liv left him.

He sits at his desk, pulling up the client's files and he tries to focus on work, his mind elsewhere as he contemplates how Liv had told him that it was over. The words had been carefully chosen and had sounded poetic, yet it was the look that she gave him that had upset him.

In their short time together, most of Liv's looks were of affection and he had never experienced such a cold look from someone who professed to love him. He had felt like a child, and he wondered what he had done to make Liv so angry, especially as he sees himself as a man with soul. He looks around the office realizing that he could never tell the other lawyers what had happened because in the logical world of legislation, feelings were not a topic of discussion. He looks around again and senses that in the sea of people, he is invisible.

Miles gets out of his chair, and very quietly closes the door to his office. It is easy to do because his secretary is gone. Her son has contracted the virus, and she is awaiting her test results.

After closing the door, he gets back in his seat and browses through therapist names on his cellphone, trying to find someone who will take his health insurance. Relying on the ratings allotted to each of the therapists, he eventually chooses a woman who is described as thoughtful and insightful. She appeals to his lawyer mind, and it reminds him of Molly, a woman whom he has just met, and he wonders what skills she brings to the therapist's office. He realizes that he is daydreaming when his door opens and one of the associates comes in to ask him a question. Quickly, he places the cellphone on his desk, hoping the associate didn't see the browsing content. In the workplace, Miles chooses to be private. Once he has answered the associate's question, he closes the door again and dials the number, making an appointment for the following day. The therapist sounds kind too and they agree to connect through the internet. The days of stretching out on a couch disappeared with the advent of the world wide web. He writes the appointment down in his book, grateful that he can meet the therapist online and, in his apartment, free from the hustle of lawyer life. Even if it is a virtual visit, it is something.

Eight

In considering the nature of those who enter lives and leave suddenly, it is prudent to acknowledge all the delights and devils that shape the human spirit. Emily is sitting with Ryan in the bar and the bartender is flirting with her, once again.

"You should dump him and run away with me," he says after Ryan retreats to the restroom. Emily smiles and doesn't say a word, choosing to twirl the straw around her old-fashioned. She looks at the bartender and smiles again, leaning in for a conspiratorial whisper.

"It's just a casual thing," she says.

"What happened to you Emily?" asks the bartender, "you seem sad."

Emily shakes her head, wanting to say something because she has known the bartender longer than all the casual flings.

"Well, you know. My dad died," she says.

"That's too bad, Emily. You should take a trip somewhere. Come with me."

"If I go anywhere, it will be with my sister. She was close to dad. It's hurting her more."

"What about your mom?"

"She likes to travel solo," says Emily, "She's a free spirit."

"Isn't she English?" asks the bartender.

Emily nods and takes another sip from her old-fashioned.

"That explains it," says the bartender and Emily smiles.

By now, Ryan has returned to his seat, and he grabs Emily's arm. He doesn't' t like the way the bartender looks at Emily. Emily resists but when she sees the look on Ryan's face, she gets off the bar stool and mouths 'bye' to the bartender. The bartender, the rival. Emily walks out of the door with Ryan, and she sways when they get outside. "I'm drunk," says Emily.

"We are getting dinner," says Ryan, keeping his grip on Emily's arm as he guides her through the streets of the Historic Third Ward, remembering a restaurant where he had enjoyed ribs with another woman one night. They go to the restaurant and read the sign on the door. Masks are no longer needed but Emily is too drunk to read the notice. She fumbles in her pocket and finds the mask, trying to put it over her mouth. She sways again, giddy with the alcohol.

"You don't need it," says Ryan, grabbing it from her hand and shoving it into his coat pocket.

"I'm scared," says Emily, trying to find stability in the middle of chaos.

They walk into the place and Ryan tells the concierge that they need a table. Emily looks around thinking that they are the only customers in the place. It is only when the server takes them to their table that she sees another couple stuck at the end of the large, open-spaced room. They seem miles away to Emily and she looks at the menu, feeling that she has seen something familiar yet disturbing. She is too drunk to recognize what she has seen. She looks at the couple again and watches the woman, walk across the room. It is her sister, Sarah.

Emily waves her arm in the air and calls out her sister's name, but her sister doesn't hear her. She tries again and Sarah swings around on her heels, finally hearing Emily. She spots her sister and freezes, because her secret is out. Sarah walks over to the table where Emily and Ryan are sitting. She walks towards them, mentally preparing her speech. It is a speech she has rehearsed several times.

"So, you are Emily's sister," says Ryan, noting the family resemblance and mentally undressing her. His jealousy game doesn't work because Emily is distracted still the worse for wear after consuming more alcohol than food. Sarah is sober, rational and scared but she gets the words out.

"I'm with one of my colleagues," says Sarah, the lie coming easily, "We are working on a big project and finished late."

More pleasantries are exchanged, and after a short interval of silence, Sarah returns to the table.

"Who is that?" asks Ian, as Sarah slides into her chair.

"My sister, Emily," she says.

"Does she know?"

Sarah shakes her head and speaks in a low voice.

"I haven't told anyone."

"Same here," says Ian, "It's easy for me being a loner. Nobody talks to me. I don't want you to get into trouble."

Sarah looks at him and feels a wave of love that hits her in the stomach, making her want to run away with him to a far-off place, where they can never be found.

She wonders how she ever got into this mess and remembers all the nights when Sam, her husband, was working late, and she stayed late at the office with Ian. She had never intended to have an affair: it had happened without planning or foresight. Now, she is in the thick of it and she has fallen for a man who is just like her. Someone who works hard but knows how to play too. Sarah watches her sister walk to the restroom with a stagger and realizes that Emily has drunk more liquor than usual. Sarah has never seen Emily so intoxicated. Somewhere in the middle of grief, Emily lost her refined essence. Suddenly, Sarah wants to get out of the restaurant, feeling embarrassed because it won't be long before Emily sobers up.

"I want to leave," she says.

"Good idea," says Ian.

They walk out of the restaurant, and Sarah feels the sense of danger again rush through her arteries, making her heart pound fast. She clutches hold of Ian's hand, feeling comfort in his presence yet knowing that it won't be long before the truth comes out because it always does.

She looks at him and feels the need to throw caution to the wind. All the time, she is wondering if it is love or merely infatuation and she doesn't have the answer to this because she is caught in the emotions of desire and loss. It is starting to hit her that her father has gone, and she will never see him again. She presses Ian's hand when they reach her car and he kisses her on the cheek, because they are in public. He has always been aware that she is a married woman. Yet as far as he is concerned, she should be with him.

"I'll see you tomorrow," he says, smiling at Sarah.

She lowers her mask and kisses him on the lips.

"I'll be glad when we can burn these damn things," she says.

Sarah drives home with her hands clutching the wheel, feeling the tension flood her body as she considers what will happen if Sam, her husband, discovers that she is having an affair. In her mind, the various scenarios play out because although Sam has never been angry with her, she knows there is the potential.

She has made sure she doesn't do anything to irritate him. Moreover, because of his job, there have been many occasions that they pass without touching each other. She has found affection in the arms of another, and she wonders how Ian really feels about her or whether for him it is just a fling with an attractive co-worker. Something in her heart tells her that it means more to him than she realizes or cares to know. She parks the car in the garage and enters the house. It is 8pm and still early but Sarah is tired. Sam has not returned from the hospital and all the various scenarios fade from her mind. She gets undressed, changes into her nightwear, and gets into the large king-size bed that she bought with Sam when they had just married. It seems like a long time ago and she wonders where the time has flown. She had known at the time that it was going to be difficult being a doctor's wife, but she had thought that everything would be fine. Now, she finds herself in the arms of another, and it is breaking her heart.

She isn't the only one who is having problems sleeping. Back in his apartment, Miles is tossing and turning remembering the good times with Liv. He feels so abandoned.

Every day, Liv brought him honey and he placed the honey in his tea or bowl of oatmeal. She loved him in little ways, and he appreciated it as many older men do, because he was wise to the ways of women and how things can be. And now, he feels foolish and has the innocence of a child because his understanding of women is challenged. Eventually, he gets back to sleep and when he wakes up, dresses and goes into the office, his mind is dazed, and he tries to concentrate but he knows that he needs help. He looks at his calendar and realizes that it is the day to see his new therapist and he relaxes, feeling that he is in good hands even if it is a virtual visit. Bright and early at 9am. The relationship with Liv is the first thing that they talk about. Miles talks to the therapist about the magical moments he shared with Liv, and how she abruptly ended the relationship. The therapist uses one word to describe the situation and the mess that he is in.

"Narcissist," says the therapist.

"I'm familiar with the term," says Miles, "I think she was tired of me."

"Narcissists tend to move on quickly once their needs are satisfied," says the therapist.

"Well, I'm not sure," says Miles, "she was very loving. I'm quite dull. I think she wanted more."

"Narcissists can show love, until they have had enough."

"You mean they can't love?" says Miles, understanding the meaning of the words.

"They need love, but they are unable to return it. It's an illusion they create. I'm sure she was persuasive," says the therapist.

Feeling very uncomfortable after the therapy session, Miles sits in his chair contemplating the trajectories in his life and he rustles through his wallet, hoping to find some distraction. It isn't long before he finds her card. The card that shows her name in big bold letters. Molly is a beautiful woman. She was kind to him, and he thinks back to their meeting in the café, needing to see her again.

"Maybe it's me who is the narcissist," thinks Miles, as he dials Molly's number. A few hours later, they are back in the café, sipping coffee. It is as if they have never left and Miles tells Molly about his therapy session.

"Was it your first therapy session?" asks Molly

"I went after I divorced," says Miles, "The man just wanted to talk about Gore."

"Al?"

"Please don't call me that," says Miles, and he winks at Molly, and she laughs. Miles looks at her again, appreciating her sense of humor. For all her loving acts, Liv was more serious than humorous.

Molly laughs again and Miles looks at the glistening in her eyes.

"So, you were telling me about your therapy session," says Molly, "Please tell me more. Did you like the therapist?"

Miles nods and stirs his coffee, glancing up and seeing the blue of Molly's eyes.

"It wasn't easy. The therapist thinks that Liv is a narcissist."

"Do you?"

"When we first met, I inundated her with gifts," says Miles, thinking back to the early days of the relationship. He had bought Liv a beautiful shawl, paintings for her condominium, and there had also been trips.

A trip to see the musical Hamilton in Chicago and an all-expenses trip to Costa Rica, where she had marveled at the sights and sounds of all the birds. Miles had tried zip-lining for the first time. She had watched with a cold look on her face. Even then, there had been signs.

"I'm familiar with narcissism," says Molly, "In fact, my dissertation was the development of a new measure of narcissism."

"I think it's me. Too much gift-giving. Isn't that what

narcissists do?" asks Miles

Molly looks at him with a bemused look on her face.

"Did you leave her after sending her all the gifts?"

"No, she dumped me," says Miles and smiles when he looks at Molly's face.

"I think you have your answer," says Molly.

"I feel stupid," says Miles.

"You seem quite intelligent to me," says Molly, "and kind too."

Miles blushes at the compliment and looks at Molly's face in a way that makes her look down at her cup of coffee.

"So are you," he says.

"Was the therapist kind to you?" asks Molly, diverting the topic to more practical matters.

"Yes, although it was virtual. It was fine but I prefer face-to-face. She explained the difference between overt and covert narcissists."

"Yes, the covert narcissists are more difficult to detect," says Molly, "They aren't as obvious because they do lots of good things."

"Liv is very altruistic. Involved in so many charities. The homeless, refugees, the mentally ill, the church."

"Gosh, she was very giving. How did she give to you?"

"There were many compliments. Especially early on. She told me that I was the love of her life."

"So, you asked her to marry you, and she said yes."

"Yes, and then she dumped me. Not one of my proudest

moments," says Miles.

Miles thinks back to the evening in Liv's condominium when he had proposed and the look of delight in Liv's face. Had it all been a farce? A look of anguish sweeps across his face as he remembers the evening and the break-up.

He stands up and feels dizzy, so he clutches hold of the chair, reaching out to Molly in a moment of panic. She reaches out to him, grabbing his arm to steady him and she sees a haze cloud his eyes, as he reaches for reality, too torn by the trauma that occurred. Finally, he steadies himself and looks at Molly in appreciation because she has helped him again. There is a delicate balance between reality and imagination when Molly touches him again and he imagines what it would have been like if he had met her instead of Liv. Of the two women, Molly is the most beautiful, yet he can't get the image of Liv out of his mind.

"I slept with her every night," says Miles, "We were like husband and wife."

"A terrible ordeal for you," says Molly.

Miles doesn't say a word and instead grabs Molly's arm, and they walk out of the coffee shop and into blazing, bright sunlight.

"I was dying in there," says Miles, "the heat."

"It was quite warm," says Molly, "no air-conditioning."

Molly squints and looks down the street, wondering if she will see her daughter, yet feeling scared that she will see Sarah with the stranger again. Because, deep down, she knows that it was her daughter and not a woman who looks like Sarah. The mind likes to play tricks. She takes a quick look and there is nobody there. Feeling the strain lift, she turns towards Miles, and he kisses her quickly and Molly is taken by surprise because it is not a kiss of friendship; it is a kiss of romance. She feels his tongue caress her mouth and the taste of caffeine swirls in her mouth like a warm embrace. Forgotten is the trauma and the losses: in one moment, they are together. They break away from each and Miles studies Molly's face, looking for a sign of resistance but there is none. He clasps Molly in a moment of peace and the sky lights up for him. Eventually, they release each other. He smiles at Molly and nods when she suggests.

"Let's take a walk along the lakefront. It's pleasant now."

They watch the waves billow as they walk along the path, not knowing what to say to each other but enjoying the time together. Molly looks at Miles thinking about his kiss, savoring the moment of togetherness. The fledgling romance turns into reality. Miles' phone buzzes and he takes the phone out of his pocket and glances at it.

"A client," he says, looking at Molly and he grimaces.

Miles stops for a moment to answer the phone. He listens and looks at Molly, wondering what it would be like to see her in bed with him, his arm holding her tight. He focuses on the client's needs and tells him that it will be easy to arrange.

"One of my clients wants to send her grandchild a gift."

"For how much?"

"Five thousand dollars."

"That's a lot for a child," says Molly, her eyes widening like an infant in a gift store. Miles thinks of a suitable gift for Molly and wonders if it would be too much.

"The client is a wealthy widow."

"A drop in the ocean."

"I guess so," says Miles and places the phone back in his pocket.

"Do you need to go into work?"

"Yes. I'm sorry," he says, "But I'd like to see you again."

"I'm around. I'm going back to work next week. To see my clients," says Molly.

"I'm sure they are more interesting than mine," says Miles.

They walk back to their cars and Miles kisses Molly on the cheek when they leave. For this, Molly is glad because she felt some guilt when he kissed her, particularly as Michael is still on her mind and she suspects that Liv is very much on Miles' mind. She wonders if he still loves her, and she is unsure of what to do. She gets into the car and drives home slowly and the voice in her head speaks to her. The voice belongs to her inner critic and sometime friend. It is time to take two big steps backwards because there is nothing between you and Miles, the inner critic tells her. It is best to heal. It is the voice that tells her not to take a risk.

Nine

Miles is sitting in his one-bedroomed apartment, and he looks at his belongings. The items that he had left at Liv's place were packed into boxes, ready for him to collect.

He thinks back to the abrupt break-up, confused about what happened and still trying to understand the reason for Liv's actions. At the same time, he thinks about his conversation with Molly and the new therapist. Narcissism. He's seen the quality in some of his colleagues but this time he is not an observer. The brute force of what has happened hits him as he sits in the living room, and he feels a wave of emotions. Sadness, hurt, and pain. He thinks of all the things that he did for Liv, and he thinks about the things that she did for him. After years of living alone, he met someone who made him feel special. Had it been a fantasy or a realization on Liv's part that they were not compatible? He wants to know and feels a compulsion. The thoughts rattle in his mind forcing him to rise from his seat and call Liv. Part of him knows that he is doing the wrong thing, but he can't control himself. Miles is surprised when Liv answers the phone at once and the sound of her voice makes him hesitate, but he presses on.

"Can I come over?" asks Miles, "I want to talk about us."

"If you must," she says and Miles winces at the coldness in

Liv's voice. Still, he is fired up and ready to see her.

"I'll be there soon," says Miles.

He puts on his coat and rushes out of the apartment, mentally rehearsing all the things that he wants to say and all the questions that he wants to ask her. Liv owns a townhouse in Fox Point, an area north of Milwaukee and he drives there thinking of all the walks that they enjoyed together. Although not a runner, Liv likes to keep in shape and her legs are muscular, slim and firm. As he drives to Fox Point, Miles thinks of the beauty of her smile when she pressed small gifts into his hands. It is a nightmare to think that she has gone, and he hopes that there is some closure or, even better, a reunion where she changes her mind. Mindful of his speed, he puts his foot on the brake, trying to calm his mind yet failing because he is almost at her place. In his fantasy, he returns to her arms. Consequently, when he parks outside the townhouse and sees a new car in the driveway, he is perplexed because Liv always enjoys driving her run-down car. He hesitates before he rings the doorbell, wondering whether she will answer. The door opens and Liv is not there. Standing in the doorway is a stranger. A tall African American man who reminds Miles of someone and he can't place him.

"You need to go," says the man, "Liv doesn't want to see you."

"But I wanted to talk," says Miles, stepping up on the doorstep. It isn't long before he hears more footsteps and Liv comes to the door.

"Don't tell me how to live my life Miles," she says

"I don't understand," says Miles, "I wanted you to be happy."

"You have your son and all your friends. Enjoy your life," says Liv and she gives him the cold look again.

Miles steps backwards down the steps, almost losing his grip. Liv looks at him with contempt and everything that he hoped would happen, breaks into a thousand pieces. He realizes that the relationship is over, and he doesn't know what to do, except to go home and look at the television because that is the only thing that exists for him right now. He drives home and his mind is blank. It is over and he wants to recover. He climbs into his queen-sized bed and falls into a deep sleep full of dragons and demons.

When he wakes up, it is early morning, and he thinks of the woman in his dream. Despite the trouble with Liv, it is a woman he thinks of often and he wonders how it would feel to be with her. Molly is a very beautiful woman. Something started between them, but he is unsure how it will progress. Is this another start of heartbreak?

Molly wakes up early too and she lies in the large king-size bed, and she thinks about Miles, and she wants to see him again and it makes her nervous. She gets out of bed and walks into the bathroom looking at the sparkle in her cheeks and thinking of the kiss that they shared. It wasn't a friendly peck on the cheek. It was a full lingering kiss that warmed her heart. Feeling like a teenager, she touches her stomach and thinks about the way that Miles touched her. She takes a deep breath, and blinks, peering into the mirror again to wash her face.

She is alone in the house, and she tenses when she hears a voice in the bathroom right behind her. Abruptly, she turns around and there is nothing there. She shakes her head knowing that she has had a hallucination. It might have been auditory, but it was as real as any ghostly specter in the night.

Only this time, it is early morning, and she is due to return to work to see all her clients. Molly splashes her face with water and pats her skin dry with a towel. She walks into the bedroom, gets dressed, and looks around the room.

"There is something you can do Molly," she says to herself, "Leave this place and start again."

There are so many memories ingrained in the rooms. Times spent with Michael when their daughters were growing up. All the Thanksgiving dinners when Michael carved the turkey; the trip to London to celebrate a wedding anniversary before the birth of their first child; the joy of the births and the first steps. So many happy memories yet when she thinks back, she feels Michael's distance too. His lateness to the birth of Sarah, as the doctor held her hand and the absences from so many moments in their daughters' lives. But most of all, Michael was absent from her. She tries to remember the last time that they made love, and she recalls a night with too much wine and food. Michael seemed young that night yet the following day, he was back to his normal self.

It was she who had drunk too much, had savored the taste of the tiramisu bought from a favorite Milwaukee bakery. Her daughters had observed all the activities with the carefree spirit of youth yet they might have sensed that something was wrong. That the public image of a happy couple was a façade for longing and loneliness? If so, they had never said anything. Instead, they had chosen to live their lives in ways that were unique.

Molly isn't the only one who is thinking. Sarah is wide awake while Sam, her husband, sleeps peacefully beside her. Sarah looks at Sam breathing with his mouth slightly ajar, and she feels a wave of concern. She rolls over to turn away from him, feeling the guilt of the affair hit her body. Moreover, there is no sign that the affair is ending and for the two lovers, it has become more intense. Like a rollercoaster on a never-ending ride of highs and lows. Sarah gets out of bed and walks into the bathroom, closing the door and she looks at herself in the mirror for a moment, knowing that she is a young and beautiful woman because she's been told this so many times yet right now, she feels like a failure.

All the good looks in the world can't repair the damage. The sunlight is shining in the bathroom and Sarah peers out drawn to Mother nature. Without hesitation, she picks out her running clothes from the chest of drawers, making sure to open and close them quietly so that Sam doesn't wake up. She tucks her cell phone into her pocket and sprints out of the door, youth giving her the ability to speed rather than cruise. After completing two miles in under eighteen minutes, she turns around and zooms back to the condominium, increasing her speed until she pants. She stops and opens her cellphone, finding a message from Ian that makes her smile.

"I miss you."

Without hesitation, she texts back.

"I miss you too."

She slips the cellphone back into her pocket and walks into the condominium that is still quiet and peaceful. She walks into the kitchen and Sam is there, sitting in his bathrobe and sipping coffee. She jumps, because she is startled to see him.

"How was your run?" he asks, and she thinks of the text messages on her phone, mentally scrubbing the contents and wondering what Sam would say if he ever saw the texts.

"It was good. I sped up towards the end."

Sam smiles and returns to his cellphone, reading all the messages from the hospital to tell him about the day's schedule so he knows what to expect. One message grabs his attention because it's the first time he has dealt with a patient with such a rare condition. Sarah walks past him, glancing at Sam's phone but there are no texts from attractive nurses or administrators. She brushes her arm against him hoping for some reaction, but Sam keeps reading his messages and preparing for his next shift.

"I'm going to shower," she says, and Sam finally looks up at her and smiles. Sarah pauses for a moment, hoping for Sam to touch her yet he returns to his cellphone and pours another cup of coffee, caught in the start of another workday.

A doctor ready to visit patients, to diagnose, to medicate, to give patients the best treatment. Yet he is unaware that Sarah is enjoying her time in the arms of another. And Sarah knows this and when she washes herself in the shower, she tries to rid herself of the guilt and shame that are part of her day. She doesn't know how she became this way.

Emily is still asleep, and when the light wakes her up, she has no hangover, and she is alone. She stays in her bed for a while thinking about the day ahead and thinking of what she can do because there is no client to see or paperwork to complete. It is over with Ryan, and she thinks of all the possibilities of how to progress with her romantic life. The desire to embark on yet another casual fling seems alien to her, and she wonders where her desire has gone.

She walks into the kitchen and fills the percolator with water. She stands on her tiptoes and reaches for her favorite coffee from Jamaica, remembering her vacation there with one of the many bar encounters. The vacation had ended the fling, and she thinks about returning there, maybe with Sarah this time. They have an amicable relationship and Sarah chooses to leave her alone most of the time, not overly concerned about her younger sister's lifestyle. It is 10am and she picks up her cellphone, choosing to phone because she feels lonely and wants to hear Sarah's voice.

"I thought I'd call you," says Emily, "I'm thinking about a vacation to Jamaica. Can you come?"

Sarah sighs and thinks about all the work that she has to do and all the time that she would miss with Ian if she went away.

"I'd love it but it's too busy at work right now."

"I remember seeing you with your colleague."

There is an awkward pause as Sarah tries to find the right words, yet she realizes that Emily, despite her casual ways, has probably guessed that there is more to the relationship than a formal work partnership.

"Ian is a good friend," says Sarah

"Are you happy Sarah?" asks Emily

"Of course. Why do you ask?"

"I just wondered about you and Sam."

"We've been married five years," says Sarah, with a defensive tone in her voice.

Emily quickly drops the topic realizing she is broaching a sensitive issue. She continues to talk about Jamaica and what they could do together.

"You should go," says Sarah, "You could do a solo trip. Didn't you go to Paris on your own?"

"Mais oui" says Emily, thinking of Notre Dame and the walks along the river. Jamaica seems extreme and she thinks of a destination that is closer to Milwaukee. Mexico.

"Mexico might be best," says Emily to her sister.

"How is your Spanish?" asks Sarah

"It's good," says Emily, thinking of one of her casual flings with a Latin lover.

The idea of travel appeals to Emily, and she stretches her arms into the air, relieved that Ryan isn't coming into the kitchen to touch her. The relief turns into sadness when she considers the fling and how it had been different, despite his careless ways.

Yet, she also realizes that she didn't really know him, just like her father. The thought of her dad triggers an emotion in her body, and it hits her with a sudden bang. She grabs hold of the kitchen surface to steady herself, glad that the conversation with her sister is over.

Her sister has a secret. Because even though her sister hasn't said a word, she remembers the glow on her face. She hasn't seen her sister look that way in a very long time. The morning turns into lunchtime and life is moving on. After eating a sandwich filled with tuna and slices of English cucumber, Molly decides. She walks around the house one more time mentally choosing furniture that she wants to keep. She picks up her cellphone and calls a realtor who is rated as one of the top performers in Milwaukee. The young woman had helped Sarah and Sam buy their condominium. It has been so long since she has been a seller in the Milwaukee region, that her knowledge of whom to contact is limited. She trusts her daughter's choice. The realtor answers the phone at once and Molly tells her what she wants.

"I want to sell my house and buy a condo," she says.

"Where would you like to live?" she says.

"Near the Oriental cinema," says Molly, "I like the area."

They arrange to meet so the realtor can appraise Molly's house.

"The inventory is low," says the realtor, "Your house will be in demand."

The realtor looks around Molly's house and makes a few suggestions though saying that it is perfect as it is.

"I'm surprised you are selling," says the realtor, "It's such a lovely place."

"Well, it's a little big for me now," says Molly, not wanting to tell her about Michael and what happened only a few weeks previously. She is still finding it difficult to tell anyone although she has told Miles about the sudden heart attack. She wonders if she will have the courage to tell him more. After the realtor leaves, Molly sits on the couch thinking about all her options. For the first time in her life, she is truly alone yet she doesn't feel lonely.

The weather is warm, and Molly feels a sudden urge to go for a run and to think about everything including her feelings for Miles. She can't understand why she still feels so drawn to him because it seems ridiculous to feel for someone else after losing a spouse; they devoted over twenty years of their lives to each other, and she barely knows Miles. She laces up her shoes wondering why she is still thinking about him. It was only a kiss, yet it had meant something to her. She suspects it meant something to him.

Meanwhile, Miles is sitting in the coffee store thinking about his life and wondering why he made such a terrible mistake in losing his heart and sanity to Liv, a woman who is now with another. Like most men, he has had his moments of jealousy yet the rage inside of him is more pronounced this time. It is not a comfortable feeling for him, and he pushes his coffee away. He looks out of the window and in a moment of serendipity he sees Molly running along the road and the world stops again.

Ten

The realtor places the sign in front of Molly's house. The open house is between 10am and noon and the realtor is confident that Molly will get an offer. The potential buyers arrive, parking their cars in front of the house. Some are masked, some are not because despite the spikes in Covid, some prefer to live as they were before the pandemic. Some want to take a risk, and the realtor hopes that one of the families will take a risk on a house that needs updating.

While the realtor tries to sell Molly's house, Molly is driving around the Lower East Side area thinking about where she wants to live. She concentrates on driving, yet her mind is elsewhere thinking about selling the house and starting a new life. The tension is in her face, and she tries to relax when she pulls up outside a condominium building that is close to the cinema where she enjoys watching foreign movies that remind her of Europe. In all the years that she has lived in the country of big dreams, her eccentricities and habits are still conventionally English. She puts on her mask, aware that she doesn't really need to don a mask because places are opening back up after the wave of delta has slowed down. She puts on the mask out of habit rather than fear because her clients are susceptible to disease due to their problems in navigating life.

Feeling bold, she steps into the condominium and introduces herself to the listing agent. The agent smiles when she hears Molly's voice.

"What brings you to Milwaukee?" she asks

"I've lived here for a long time. I'm looking to downsize."

"The kids have flown the nest?" asks the agent.

Molly nods going along with the harmless lie because there don't have to be any explanations. The agent hands Molly her card, and Molly walks around the condominium noting the updates in the kitchen complete with a gas cooker and a stainless-steel refrigerator that is fit for a family. Molly strokes the cat that is sitting on the sofa and contemplates the notion of having a pet of her own; Michael had never wanted one. He had argued that it was too much work to have a dog, and he was not partial to cats, considering them too elusive. Molly's mother had liked cats and Molly thinks of the elusive but constant affection of the tabby that her mother had loved. Feeling motivated by the thought of a furry friend, Molly strides around the condominium realizing that it is too large for herself and a feline companion, but she enjoys the tour of the palace. It is a palace, and it isn't her. She likes the feel of an old place complete with creaky floorboards and windows that don't shut properly. Of course, it would just be her and she thinks about Miles and how he seems to fit the ideal of a good man in an old home. A man with lines around his eyes and a face that has experienced things. A man she could trust.

Wanting to see him again, she drives to the coffee shop and walks in, her face falling when she discovers he isn't there. She wonders if he has reunited with his fiancée after the lover's tiff. Pushing aside disappointment, she orders a cappuccino and glances at the biscotti, deciding to resist temptation. She walks over to a table near the window, looking outside hoping to see Miles strolling by. She wants to call him, but her timidity stops her, and she frowns at her lack of assertiveness in dealing with romantic encounters. She walks out of the coffee shop and walks across the road to the park to pass the time before the open house finishes. Molly admires the flowers that adorn the garden beds, and she watches a young couple with their toddler walking down to the pavilion. Feeling calm entering her body, she glances at her watch and heads back to the car. She drives home and the realtor is there to greet her, and she is smiling.

"We are about to get an offer," she says, looking at her cellphone, "It's a married couple with two children. Both doctors. They might offer cash. Their agent is texting me now."

"That's wonderful," says Molly, her face lighting up at the news.

"I'll stay in touch," says the realtor and Molly walks back into the house feeling ready for the rest of the day. She sits down on the sofa and takes out her cellphone, cursing because the battery has died and needs charging. She plugs the phone into the charger and the cellphone springs to life. There are several emails from clients who want to book a therapy session or who need to share what is happening in their lives, and it takes a moment for her to read them. She looks at the cellphone again realizing that she has missed something. She adjusts her reading glasses and there it is. It is a text message from Miles, and it is brief and succinct.

"How are you, Molly? Give me a call. I'd like to see you."

Without hesitation, she dials his number. His voice is gentle and soft, and she relaxes remembering the stillness in his smile. They talk for a moment, and she tells him about the house.

"I might get an offer today," says Molly.

"That's terrific. Do you have time to see me?"

"I'm free today. I have a client tomorrow, but my week is slow. Just getting back into the swing of things. How about you?"

"Are you free for dinner tonight?"

"I'd enjoy that," says Molly feeling impetuous and bold because she normally makes plans several days in advance.

"Is there somewhere you'd like to go?"

"I like sushi," says Molly and smiles when Miles confesses that he has a passion for sashimi.

"I'll make a reservation for seven. I can pick you up," says Miles.

Molly puts down the phone, feeling like an excited teenager in a mature body. She thinks back to an old flame from college who had kissed her in a similar fashion but who had only one thing on his mind. It had been a time of high hormones with little commitment. Molly's day unfolds with a series of positive events. The realtor calls and tells her that the couple have made an official offer with earnest money placed in the account. The closing is in thirty days and Molly suddenly panics, realizing that she has nowhere to go. She thinks about what to do and considers the place that she saw on the Lower East Side. It was too big for her, but she feels confident that there are other smaller places in the area. Feeling her panic rising, she calls the realtor back.

"Good to hear from you again Molly."

"I'm just realizing that I need to find somewhere to live. Can you help me?"

They talk and the realtor promises Molly that she will send her a choice of condos in the neighborhood. After the brief discussion, Molly feels the calm enter her body and she thinks about her dinner with Miles. She can deal with the selling and buying process tomorrow. Tonight, she has a date, and she is excited. He arrives at seven and rings Molly's doorbell. By now, Molly has calmed herself through laughing at her adolescent emotions. Her rational mind tells her that neither of them are ready to be in a relationship; there is too much healing to be done. Her heart is beating rapidly when she looks at him again and logic disappears. And so, they go out to a restaurant close to Molly's house.

"Do you know this place?" asks Miles, as he opens the door

for her like an old-fashioned southern gentleman.

Molly shakes her head and walks into the restaurant because it's a long time since a handsome man has taken her out on a date. They settle into the booth and Miles leans over with the menu.

"You can choose," he says.

Molly looks at the menu and suggests some dishes that she likes. She looks at him and appraises his good looks. Miles is quite the catch, and she wonders why his fiancée said goodbye. She watches him run his fingers through his hair and she notices the tired look on his face.

"How have you been Miles?" she asks and leans forward, wanting to help but unsure of what to do. He looks at her and senses that Molly has detected that things haven't been going so well. He has managed to get some sleep but when he has slept there have been nightmares normally including Liv and her new man.

"I've been tired," he says, "The clients have needed a lot of paperwork done."

"It's not an easy job," says Molly.

"Well, your job is more difficult than mine. I just prepare the tax documents. You listen to people's real problems."

Molly nods her head wondering how she can encourage him to speak about his own problems, but she focuses on ordering dinner, hoping that the connection between them will create some moments of transparency.

Miles reaches across the table and touches Molly's hand. She smiles at the intimacy, and her hand stays in place. The touch is brief, and Miles withdraws his fingers from her soft skin. Miles is poised and polished in public, but Molly can sense that his thoughts and feelings are jumbled. She can see it in his face.

"It's good to see you Molly," he says, hesitating in his words, "I've been a mess."

"Well, you've been through so much," says Molly.

"It seems trivial compared to your tragedy."

"You can talk to me," says Molly.

"I went around to see Liv. To get some explanation."

"How was she?" asks Molly

"Surprisingly happy. She wished me well."

"A little strange," says Molly.

"That's what I thought. It seemed unreal."

"Well, as I told you. Narcissists can be very charming," says Molly. She smiles at him, and he feels the warmth of her kindness. He wonders what is wrong with him. Why is he still torn about a woman who abandoned him?

"I keep forgetting you wrote about narcissism," says Miles and he finds himself smiling too because there is something very positive about Molly and he realizes that he likes her. In fact, it would be fair to say that the feeling is erotic because she is a very beautiful woman. A woman to remember. The lights in the restaurant are dim and Molly and Miles move closer towards each other, discovering each other without saying a word.

"You can talk to me about her," she says.

Miles looks into Molly's eyes and appreciates her honesty and beauty.

"I feel lost," he says, "Yet at the same time, I feel some relief."

"Why do you feel relief? she asks.

"I don't understand why but I think it's because you are right. That she is a narcissist. And my therapist thinks so too."

"I don't always get it right," says Molly, "In fact, quite often, I get it wrong."

By now, the food has arrived, and the pair dip the sashimi into the soy sauce, feeling the sexual tension growing between them. Miles continues his story and Molly is eager to hear. She wants to understand what happened to him.

"I went to see her again," says Miles, "A man opened the door. He told me that she didn't want to see me."

"Another man," says Molly, "She moved on quickly. What a terrible thing."

"It was strange because as soon as he spoke, she came to the door to speak to me. It felt like a game."

"Yes, very bizarre. Game-playing is what they do best," says Molly.

"Have you ever been tricked by a narcissist?" asks Miles.

Molly thinks about her encounters over the years with academics, clinicians and clients.

"I don't think I've been tricked," she says, "But I've encountered a few. I try to stay away from them."

"I think she lined him up while she was with me," says Miles, thinking of the handsome African American man who had opened the door.

"Is she good-looking?" asks Molly, feeling a tinge of jealousy and not liking herself for the feeling.

"It was her smile. It lit up her face," says Miles. "I liked the way she spoke. She was cultured."

"What does she do for a living?" asks Molly.

"She was an instructor at the community college. She retired a few years ago."

"It must have been nice to have someone care for you after you had a long day at work," says Molly.

"She did a lot of volunteering. We ate out a lot," says Miles.

"Oh, I see. She's generous in public. Does a lot of good things" says Molly.

"Yes, but not so much at home. Well, she did cook some meals. She talked a lot about herself and her dreams."

"What about your dreams?"

"I tried to make her happy," says Miles.

Miles frowns and looks at Molly, seeing the blueness in her eyes. Like Liv, Molly is fair, yet she is more youthful than his former fiancée and there is a kindness in her eyes that is permanent. She seems like a genuine person unlike the changing faces of Liv, his covert narcissist.

"Do you have any advice for me Molly? I'm sure as a clinician you hear these types of stories all the time."

"I do hear some terrible things," she says, thinking of all the times she has tossed and turned in bed after hearing of other people's nightmares.

She pauses for a moment thinking of words of comfort and advice.

"I'm glad that you are looking after yourself," she says. "One of the things that seems to help my clients is facing what happened."

"Going back to the scene of the crime, you mean," says Miles.

"From a detective standpoint, it most certainly helps," says Molly and they laugh together. Miles thinks for a moment and then an idea seizes him.

"It's very risky but we could go to the Pfister Hotel."

"The Blu room?" asks Molly

"That's where Liv and I met for our first date," says Miles, "Do you fancy a nightcap?"

"Why not?" says Molly and Miles pays for the food and they quickly walk out of the restaurant and head for his car.

"Let's do it without hesitation," says Molly and they quicken their pace.

They walk into the foyer of the Pfizer hotel and Molly looks up at the ceiling that is adorned with cherubs, and she imagines herself flying with the cherubs across the expanse of the hotel ceiling. She brings herself back to reality and Miles is looking at her.

"You lost me for a moment," she says, and they quickly walk towards the elevator that takes them all the way up to the Blu room. It is the perfect place for a nightcap, and they find a table quickly because despite the lifting of the lockdown, most people are choosing to stay indoors. They both order scotch and Molly smiles when she takes the first sip, feeling the warmth of the liquor slide down her throat.

"I don't know many women who take their scotch neat," says Miles.

"Do you know many English women?"

"Not really," says Miles, "I met a couple who are English. I am friends with a woman who introduced them to me."

"Most of my friends are American," says Molly.

They are quiet for a moment as Miles considers the state of things and how he feels about being back in the place where they first met. When he first met Liv.

Eleven

It is the morning after and Molly wakes up in bed alone, thinking of her dinner with Miles. She remembers the good food, the wine and the way that Miles looked at her after the evening had ended.

Yet again, she feels like a foolish teenager. She gets out of bed and checks her cellphone, hoping for a text from him. But there is nothing and the excitement fades as she considers her age and her responsibilities. It seems that a new romance awaits her, yet she is healing. Miles hasn't been cautious. He flew over to her place like a passionate lover. There is no sign that he wants to take it slow yet she feels caught in a frenzy of emotions and she wants to be sensible. Not the giggling, foolish adolescent girl that she once was. She feels unsure of the connection and realizes that she needs someone's advice. Not a therapist but an old friend and she thinks of Betty, whom she last saw at the retirement party. Betty had encouraged her to stay in touch and Molly digs out her phone number, choosing to text rather than phone because of the early hour. "Are you free for dinner?" she types, "I need some advice."

It isn't long before Betty responds, and they arrange to meet at a tapas place that Betty favors. The day passes and the evening arrives and when Molly sees Betty, she realizes that she has missed seeing her every day at college.

Once they have taken their seats and chosen an array of small plates, Betty touches Molly's arm and tells her that she looks good.

"What advice can I give you?"

"I've met someone Betty. It happened just after Michael's death. It's the strangest thing because I barely know him, yet I really enjoy his company. It seems authentic. He's had a tough time too. He was due to marry someone, and she called it off."

"When did the engagement end?" asks Betty.

"Not long ago. It seems rushed for him to start a new relationship."

"I have to agree," says Betty.

Molly runs the fingers through her hair, and she yawns.

"Am I that boring?" asks Betty, with a twinkle in her eye.

"I'm sorry. I had a late night."

"Where did he take you?"

"It was sushi and a night cap at the Blu room."

The two women laugh.

"Are you feeling better now Molly?"

"I am. Much better. You helped."

"I know a woman who was married for forty years. He died a couple of years ago. Before Covid."

"Thank goodness. There's been enough lives lost."

"They decided to get married the day after they met. She told me that she knew. I know that she was very happy with him."

"Did she date again after he died?" asks Molly.

Betty nods and smiles thinking of her friend.

"She's dating someone. He's retired, like her."

Molly feels stillness inside her body, and she is glad that she has seen Betty. However, it still doesn't answer how to deal with Miles or the feelings that she has for him. The matter is taken out of her hands when she checks her cellphone and there is a message from Miles, inviting her for lunch the following day. Without hesitating, she tells him she is looking forward to seeing him. She returns to the house and calls the agent to find out what is happening with the offer.

"They want to move in early," says the realtor, "Closing in 25 days."

"I need to find a place very quickly," says Molly.

"There is a beautiful condominium not far from where you currently live. It's about to come on the market but I can arrange a viewing before it does."

"Who owns it?" asks Molly.

"One of the realtors. She is getting married and moving in with her fiancée."

They finish the conversation and Molly feels that the world is finally on her side. She looks at the card that the therapist gave her for brainspotting and realizes that she doesn't want any fancy therapy techniques. Miles might need it more than she does, unless she is fooling herself again. The phone rings and it is Sarah, who, as usual, is checking in on her mother. Emily has disappeared and Molly has no idea what is happening in Emily's life even though she has an urge to know. Right now, she is exhausted, and Sarah wants to know what is happening in her life. It feels like parenting in reverse.

"How are things mom?"

"I've sold the house Sarah. The closing is less than thirty days away."

"But you will be homeless mom! Are you sure this is the right thing to do after everything that has happened?"

"I think I'll be fine Sarah," says Molly, feeling anxious wondering if she has been foolish to sell the house so quickly. Moreover, Miles is also a secret to her daughters although Emily probably wouldn't care. But she is sure that Sarah would frown at the timing, particularly if she heard that Miles was still in love with someone else.

"You can come and stay with us," says Sarah, "we have a spare room."

"If I don't find a place, I'll rent," says Molly, "I know you care about me Sarah. You don't need to worry."

Inwardly, Sarah breathes a sigh of relief because Molly might have found out about the affair if she had come to stay.

After talking with Sarah, Molly dials Emily's number, wondering why she hasn't heard from her youngest daughter. She wonders whether Emily has finally fallen in love. When her daughter answers the phone at once, Molly is surprised because she normally has to leave a voice mail.

"Sorry I haven't been in touch Mom," says Emily.

"I know you are busy," says Molly, "How have you been?"

"Fine. Busy with work. I'm thinking of going on a trip too."

"Oh good. You need a vacation."

"I thought I'd go to Cancun. Rent a car and drive to Tulum. See some sights. A solo trip."

"So, you are going alone," says Molly, "that's unlike you. I thought you might have some handsome man in tow."

"I'm thinking about things mom," says Emily.

"You know where I am, if you need advice. I was just calling to tell you that I've sold the house. I'm going to look for a condo on the east side."

"That's good. You need to get out of that house."

Molly puts down the phone and contemplates the state of things and how she feels. There is a shift in her family. Emily has changed from a party girl to a nomad and Sarah is anxious and she isn't sure what has happened to herself. She still feels like a foolish teenager. She doesn't have much time to think about all the events because the phone is ringing, and the sound is insistent. It's her realtor with news about the condo that is available.

"We can see it today," says the realtor, "Are you available at 3pm?"

"I am," says Molly, feeling excited because it seems that everything is falling into place. It all seems too good to be true for Molly, yet she can't help but think of Miles and the connection they have made. A few hours later, Molly and the realtor are in the condo and Molly's face is full of happiness again.

"Well, this is a good place," she says, looking at the new wooden floors that fill the living room and dining area. The bedrooms are plush with carpet, newly steamed.

"It's a two-bedroom, two-bath," says the realtor, "It's perfect for guests. There's also a small den just off the dining area."

They look at the den and Molly imagines herself typing her therapy session notes, with a cat resting on a chair next to her.

"This is perfect," says Molly, "Some of my clients prefer virtual sessions. They don't have time to drive. I'd like to make an offer. What price do you think?"

"These condominiums are very popular because of the location. It will go quickly."

"I'd like to offer more than the asking price so I can get it."

"I think that will work," says the realtor, "I'll call the agent."

The condominium is on the tenth floor and Molly looks out of the window, pleased with the view because it is not far from Lake Michigan, and she can see the boats bobbing on the waves. It is a bright and beautiful day in Milwaukee and Molly feels the electricity fill her body. It is not just the apartment or selling the family home. It is the thought of seeing Miles again because they have a date for lunch the following day. She wonders how he feels about the lunch and whether he has seen his former fiancée. She also wonders what Liv looks like and whether she would be able to detect the narcissism hidden underneath the halo.

She pushes the thought out of her mind and concentrates on immediate matters because the new place is not suitable for the current furniture that she has in the home. The old furniture is suitable for a family and belongs to the past with Michael. She will need to buy some modern-day furniture for her new life ahead. Whether Miles will be a part of it is uncertain, but she knows that she can do this alone. She can live a single life. The following morning, Molly's phone rings and it is Miles.

She feels the tension in her stomach because they have a lunch date and she wonders if he will cancel because he has things on his mind, particularly Liv. But there is no mention of Liv, and his voice is soft and gentle.

"What time shall I pick you up?" asks Miles.

"What time is the reservation?"

"For noon. How about I pick you up at 11am and we can drive around?"

"That works," says Molly, and she mentally scans her wardrobe picking out a suitable outfit for lunch. Nothing too tight or overly revealing: an outfit for a woman in her sixties. Mollys laughs because she is now in her sixties, and she is going out on a date. She feels like her single daughter Emily, who has chosen many outfits for casual dates. Molly wonders what

Emily would say if she knew about her date with Miles and she senses that Emily wouldn't really care because she is too tied up with work and her active love life.

Miles arrives promptly at 11am and parks his car outside Molly's house. He stops for a moment to admire the garden with neatly trimmed hedges and carefully chosen flowers. He looks at his hands, realizing that he has nothing to offer Molly and feels foolish that he didn't bring a bouquet.

He wonders if she likes him as much as he likes her. He casts his nervousness to one side and rings the doorbell, combing back his hair with his fingers. He can tell that it is thinning. Molly opens the door, and she looks stunning, wearing a simple blue outfit that highlights her fair hair and complexion. He realizes that she is nervous too because her face is slightly flushed. They exchange pleasantries and Miles wants to kiss her when she embraces him. Molly feels the tension in his body.

"I needed that," says Miles

"Tough week?" asks Molly.

"The clients. Some of them complained about their invoices. I hate it."

"I'm surprised you must deal with that. Isn't that a job for billing?"

"Probably. I just deal with these things."

They get in the car and Molly watches Miles drive down the road, his hands clutching the wheel.

"This is very nice," she says, and Miles stops gripping the wheel. His face relaxes as does Molly's face.

On the journey, Molly chatters away like an English school girl, telling Miles about selling the house and making an offer on a new condominium.

"Where is it?" he asks, and he is amazed when she tells him the address.

"That's only two blocks from where I live," he says.

"Well, that is a coincidence. A good one," she says, "let's hope they will accept the offer."

"When will you hear?"

"Hopefully, today," she says.

"You should keep your phone on," says Miles, "you don't want to miss it."

They arrive at the pub and Miles orders shepherd's pie while Molly favors fish and chips. After they have finished their meal, Miles pats his stomach.

"I ate too much," he says, looking at Molly's plate. She has eaten most of the fish and left a pile of French fries.

"In England, we call them chips," says Molly.

"I knew that," says Miles, "and you say biscuits rather than cookies."

Molly laughs and her eyes light up when she looks at Miles.

"Your knowledge of the British is impressive" she says.

"I already told you I'm an anglophile," he says.

They finish their meal and walk out of the pub, enjoying each other's company. And, all the while, Miles is comparing Molly to Liv and recognizes that she is very different. Molly continues her chatter and Miles looks at her face as she speaks. There is no coldness or harshness, and he wonders what he was thinking, ending up with someone like Liv. Molly is fresh, fun and, most importantly, kind. Miles spaces out for a moment imagining a different kind of life with Molly. He comes out of the trance and Molly is looking at him with a bemused look on her face.

"What are you thinking Miles?" she asks.

"Well, I was thinking about Liv", he says without checking his words. He curses himself when he watches Molly's face fall.

"Sorry, I wasn't thinking Molly."

"It's fine. I understand. It's so recent. It was a terrible thing that happened to you."

"It only lasted nine months," he says to Molly.

"How are you feeling now?"

"Right now, I feel better. But I'm still feeling bad about what happened. It doesn't help with this new man in the picture."

"I remember you told me about the new man" says Molly, "That was so quick. Who is he? Is it someone you know?"

"I don't know his name," says Miles, "He answered the door when I went over there."

"Dear me," says Molly, "How awful for you."

"There's part of me that is relieved. She talked about her past men, and it was so confusing. One minute she loved them, and the next minute they were her enemies. I wonder if any of it was true."

"They can be good liars," says Molly, "She was gaslighting you. It's a very common tool with narcissists."

There is a moment of quiet and Miles reflects on the experience. Liv is a person who hides behind a curtain of charm. She had charmed him, had claimed his heart, and then had dropped the bomb. She rejected him and moved onto the next one. He looks across the table and his face lights up when he sees Molly. Molly's warmth envelops him like a warm blanket of light. A miracle has happened to him.

"You are a wonderful person," says Miles, "I'm surprised you want to spend time with me."

"Well, to be honest, I like you," says Molly.

"Just like?"

Molly shakes her head, wanting to say more but stops herself from revealing her real feelings because it's too soon to be with another. So, she tells herself.

"You make me feel good," says Molly, "To be honest, I'm not at my best right now. I lost my husband. I'm still in shock."

"I feel selfish talking about my stuff after what happened to you. Do you want to talk more about it? What was he like?" asks Miles.

"You don't need to hear about my troubles. I'm seeing a therapist to help me," says Molly, "But I am remembering the good times. He was a good dad."

Molly looks at the ground feeling the grief. She looks at Miles after a while and sees the warmth in his face. The feelings of guilt go away. She tells herself that she hasn't suddenly replaced Michael with another man. Being with Miles feels right to her and they continue their walk, talking about other things: books, films, plays and art. After the walk has finished, Molly opens her bag and retrieves her wallet. She takes out the card and gives it to Miles.

"Brainspotting?" asks Miles, "Will this rewire my brain"?

"Probably not," says Molly, "But I've heard good things about brainspotting. It can help people who are traumatized. Our bodies hold many wounds."

"Trauma? Is that what this is for?" asks Miles.

"Trauma affects how you think or feel, and the body also holds the stress. But it can be relieved. You are probably working on yourself already. There's less tension in your face. You seem better."

"It's because I'm with you," says Miles and he kisses her gently on the lips. She returns the kiss, wanting to be with him. They embrace and Molly wraps her arms tightly around him. Miles enfolds her in his arms. Finally, they break away from each other, silent and happy.

"What else can I do Molly? To help recover?"

"You are already doing it. Keep running."

"Want to run with me sometime?'

"Yes, I'd enjoy it. The weekend always works well for me."

"How about this evening? I don't have any meetings today."

"That works too."

"I'll come to your place again. Does 6pm work?"

Molly nods and regains some equilibrium. He held her in a way that threw her off-balance. It was a good feeling.

"We can run along the lakefront. It will be light still."

Miles drops Molly back at her house and she walks inside, feeling like an excited teenager again. She sits down and her inner critic speaks to her.

"What on earth am I doing?" she says to herself.

Twelve

The run together opens all their reward systems. Their brains ignite as they occasionally glance at each other with a mischievous smile. Molly runs light and free with memories of the past stored away. It is so long that she has run with someone that Molly's face lights up despite the slower pace. Molly is naturally fast, and she dampens her desire for speed and enjoys the slowness of the run. The couple travel into Lake Park and past the concrete lions. Molly talks and points at the sky because it is almost sunset and the sun is descending into the Lake filling the water with beams of light, so beautiful that they fall silent admiring the power of nature.

Molly checks her watch after they have run a mile, glad to be running with Miles because she has a sudden memory of sprinting into Lake Park trying to catch Michael. They continue to run passing Lake Park Bistro, a renowned French restaurant, and move deeper into the park, feeling the darkness descend on them. Molly stops and looks at her watch.

"Do you want to turn around Miles?"

"How far have we come?" he asks

"A mile and a half."

"It will be three miles when we finish. I haven't run this far in months," says Miles.

They turn around and Molly slows down because she can see that Miles is struggling to keep up the pace. He stops for a moment to catch his breath and then he starts to run again.

"You go ahead of me," he says.

"Are you sure?"

Miles nods and Molly picks up the pace, glad to be running at a much faster pace than usual: she needs the quick pace because of all the recent excitement. The sellers of the condominium have accepted her offer and she will be able to move before the new people move into the old house.

Everything is settled and she runs at the speed of a jaguar, relishing every moment. She gets to the Water Tower and stops for a moment, looking back for Miles because she wants to run some more with him. She doesn't want to abandon him. She pauses her watch and looks at the cars driving up the hill towards the hospital. Immediately, her focus is on one car. It is Sarah and Molly waves, but Sarah doesn't see her. The man in the driver's seat turns and spots Molly and he slams on the brakes. The force of the breaking causes Sarah to look and her eyes connect with Molly's eyes. Almost at once, the driver accelerates, and the car is gone, leaving Molly feeling bewildered and confused because she recognizes the man from before. She thinks of all the incidents over the last few months and connects the dots. Slowly, she considers that Sarah is having an affair. She doesn't want to rush to conclusions, but the evidence is there.

Molly watches Miles run towards her, and he has picked up his pace to catch her up.

"I just saw my daughter," she says, after Miles stops to catch his breath.

"I remember that you have two daughters," he says, his hands digging into his thighs. He takes a sharp intake of breath.

"Are you ok?" asks Molly, seeing Miles gasping for breath.

"I'm fine Molly. I'm out of shape."

Miles takes another breath and relaxes, glad for the rest.

"Please tell me what happened Molly."

"It was Sarah, the eldest," says Molly, hesitating because she is unsure how to continue the conversation without revealing her worse fears.

"Did you see something bad?" asks Miles, quick to pick up the conversation because he can sense that Molly wants to speak about what she saw.

"No, nothing happened. She was with someone. I recognized him."

"So not her husband?"

"No. She's been married five years. I know Sam well. He's a doctor."

"Perhaps it is someone she works with."

"I'm sure you are right. It's just my imagination again. I worry about my daughters."

The pair continue to run, and Molly slows down so she can run next to Miles, and she feels close to him. She needs him right now, especially after seeing Sarah. She wonders what she is going to do, and she knows that she needs to talk to Sarah to find out what is happening. They finish the run and Miles asks Molly if she has plans for the evening.

"I don't have any plans. I'm just a little distracted. My brain is racing. I keep seeing Sarah with that other man. I hope it is innocent", says Molly, taking a deep breath and the adrenaline goes down.

"Anyway, I enjoyed the run," says Molly.

"So did I, "says Miles. "I need to do more. I'm really out of shape."

"You did well," says Molly, "I can tell you have some natural talent."

"Can we do it again sometime?" asks Miles.

"Of course. I am sorry about what happened on the run."

"You don't need to apologize," says Miles, "You should talk to your daughter. Find out what's going on."

"I was thinking the same," says Molly, "It's best not to avoid it. She saw me too so we can't run circles around it."

She leans towards him, looking at him with such delight that he pulls her towards him and kisses her with such vigor that she gets dizzy. Molly feels the warmth from Miles' body soothe and comfort her after the encounter with Sarah. The thought of her daughter with another man is alarming to Molly and there is a part of her that doesn't want to know the truth of the situation because she feels that everything she values will fall apart.

"I'll call you," says Miles and Molly knows that he will keep his promise. There is something about the way in which he holds himself; she feels that he is a man to trust. Miles is a man who could provide so many gifts to the right woman. Molly is unsure whether she is the woman that Miles is looking for, or any woman right now. Despite the sparkle in his eyes, he is still recovering from Liv, a woman whose light blinded him to the reality of the situation.

Molly walks into the house and goes upstairs to take a shower, thinking about what to say to her daughter without making accusations. It is inconceivable to Molly that her daughter would betray Sam, her husband. Yet, she is no fool and knows that even the most faithful women can fall for someone who turns on the charm. After the shower, she dries her hair and slips into a soft robe, thinking about Miles and the kiss on the doorstep. The memory of the kiss soothes her and gives her courage. She picks up the phone and calls her daughter. Sarah answers her cellphone straight away when she sees that it is Molly. Because of what happened. Sarah knows what is coming.

"I'm on my own mom. Sam is still at work," she says, after Molly asks if it is a good time to talk.

"I thought I saw you this evening," says Molly, "You were in a car with a man. I don't want to have an argument or make accusations. I just wanted to find out if something is wrong and how I can help."

"There's nothing wrong mom," says Sarah, "I work with Ian. We are working on a project together and it was a late night." There is a lack of conviction in Sarah's tone and Molly knows that she is not telling the whole truth.

"You don't need to be a closed book with me Sarah," says Molly, "I'm your mom. You know I love you and care about you."

Sarah grasps Molly's words because telling a lie is not how she was raised, and she feels uncomfortable.

"I'd rather talk about it face to face Mom," says Sarah, "I'm not comfortable on the phone. I want to see you. It's complicated."

"I'm sorry if I sounded harsh. You know that I worry. When can we meet?" asks Molly.

"I'm busy at work tomorrow morning. How about lunch?"

"I'll come and pick you up at one," says Molly, feeling some relief that she can address the issue with her daughter while also sensing that she will have to address some issues of her own. Molly was with Miles and although her daughter didn't see him, Sarah is probably wondering why Molly was running alone at night through the upper east side of Milwaukee.

Sarah knows that it is not her mother's style to run at night; she is a morning person who runs when it is quiet. Molly goes to bed and tosses and turns because of what has happened. It isn't only Sarah that is keeping her awake. Her mind is doing somersaults thinking about Miles and she replays the events of the week - Miles on the run and the lunch the day before.

She also wonders what is happening to her family. Emily is withdrawn and Sarah appears to be involved with another man. After a couple of hours of not falling asleep, she gets up and walks downstairs to the living room to pick up her laptop. Despite all the recent events, Molly still had time to work on the book. The editor had suggested minor changes in the development of the story and Molly has almost finished the final revision. All the minor editing is done, and the book is ready for one final review.

It is her first murder mystery, and she still can't believe that she has written it. An hour later, it is three in the morning and Molly has made the final revision with a slight plot twist to increase the tension in revealing the killer.

All that was needed was a couple of red herrings. Now the revision is made, Molly relaxes, and she closes the laptop and falls into a sleep, full of dreams of far-off lands. She is running along the beach with Miles, and they are both young, so young that they are quick and nimble. It is as if nothing can stop them until Molly trips and Miles catches her before she falls on the ground. The imaginary fall wakes her, and she yawns. It is late morning, and she overslept. She gets out of bed feeling nervous because she is seeing Sarah and will hear more about her daughter's dilemma.

When Sarah wakes up, she turns on her side and looks at Sam. Her husband is sleeping. She wonders what he will do if he finds out about Ian. She also wonders if he already knows, and she gets a horrible feeling in her stomach because she has never seen Sam get angry. She gets in the shower and washes her hair, thinking about Ian and the way that he touches her. The guilt spreads through her body as she considers all the ways in which she has been unfaithful to Sam: the emotional, social, and physical pleasures.

A few hours later she is sitting in the restaurant with her mother and the waiter hands them the menus. They engage in light talk, discussing Sarah's job and Molly's purchase of a new place to live. Once the meal is finished, Molly reaches over and touches Sarah's hand.

"It is not my place to judge you, Sarah. I know you aren't happy. Are you having an affair?"

Because of the sincerity in her mother's voice, Sarah falters and she decides to be honest.

"I can't deny it mom," she says.

"Are you happy in your marriage?" asks Molly.

Sarah runs her fingers through her hair and Molly tenses because Michael used to do the same thing when he was anxious. Sarah adopted the same habit. She is stressed too.

"Of course," says Sarah, "I love Sam."

"Are you sure? Your behavior suggests otherwise."

"Please don't accuse me mom," says Sarah, and she frowns at her mother.

"I'm not accusing you, Sarah. I reached out to you because I care about you. You are my daughter. I love you."

Sarah looks around the restaurant at the other diners and sees a young couple holding hands. They look happy and she feels jealous because she remembers how things were when she first met Sam.

"I feel awful mom. I don't know how it happened."

"It happens more often than you think," says Molly, "You can talk to me about it. I won't break your confidence."

"Do you promise?"

"Of course. I wouldn't do that to you. I told you once. I love you. I'm here to help you."

Sarah pauses again trying to think of how to start.

"How do you know him? It might help to start at the beginning," says Molly.

"We were assigned to a team project. There was one other person who got sick from Covid. It ended up with Ian and me on the team. I knew he was attracted to me. I could tell by the way he looked at me. I must admit that I was flattered. I thought he might try to love bomb me because someone did that to me when I was at college. He was different. He told me that he wouldn't touch me because I was married. I don't think either of us meant it to happen. It just did.

One night we were working late on the project, and I knew it was on both our minds. He kissed me and I let him. A few weeks later, I went back to his apartment. He lives downtown so it was easy to drop by."

"Thanks for telling me, Sarah. I know how hard it must be for you."

"Can I ask for your advice mom?"

"Of course," says Molly, "I'm here for you."

"Should I tell Sam?"

"I've always found in matters of the heart that the truth always comes out."

"I should tell him," says Sarah, "I don't want him to find out from his friends. It would be awful."

Sarah looks around the restaurant again, and the couple with love in their eyes have left. In her mind, it seems like a terrible thing to do: to tell a spouse about an affair. Yet in her heart, she knows that it is the right thing for her to do because it is Sam and even if it is the end of the marriage, she is willing to open her heart and find out if the damage can be repaired. If he can get past her mistake.

Sarah and Molly leave the restaurant and Molly returns home, thinking about her daughter and hoping that the conversation between Sarah and Sam goes well.

She doesn't have much time to think about it because as soon as she has taken off her coat, the phone rings and it is Miles.

"Can I see you?" asks Miles.

"I just got home. You can come over now, if you want," says Molly, feeling breathless at the rapid succession of events.

"Something happened," says Miles, "I'll be with you soon."

Molly checks herself in the mirror, wanting to look her best for Miles and she wonders what happened and if it was connected to Liv because what happened to him was beyond her comprehension. What happened to her was beyond her own comprehension and she brushes her thoughts of pain to one side, wanting to be there for Miles when he shows up. It isn't long before he arrives, and he confirms what she thought.

"I saw Liv," says Miles.

"Gosh, that must have been upsetting," says Molly.

"It was," says Miles, "She was with the other man. I was waiting in line for coffee, and they were ahead of me. She turned around and she saw me. She gave me such a cold look that I got out of the line and walked out of the store. I couldn't believe it."

"It seems so immature. Especially, as you were so close."

"Were we?" asks Miles, "I'm wondering now. When I was married, it felt real."

"What was it like? When you were married."

"It was good at the beginning. I realize that I never told you. My wife left me for someone else. I went to therapy and the therapist helped me heal. This seems worse."

"It's because it was so sudden. I am sorry to hear about your wife. I didn't know."

"It's a long time ago. I have a son who lives in Indiana. Something good came from the marriage. I neglected my wife because of my job. I understand why she left me."

Miles looks at Molly and thinks about her loss and how she has dealt with it.

"You are a very strong woman," he says, and he leans over and kisses her, knowing that this is the start of something strong. Something much better than before.

Thirteen

Sometimes it is worthy to speak of a grand design, yet it does not capture the sizzle that occurs when two people collide.

There is nothing planned about the occasion and no effort is needed; it is total chaos and in the moment that Miles kisses Molly in her living room, a spark is ignited just like a match thrown onto a fireplace full of wooden logs. Miles' hands touch Molly's back moving across her body and she feels the warmth of his touch. Eventually, they disengage, and Molly looks at Miles and smiles. He smiles back at her in wonder, knowing that something has happened between them.

"We should go out for dinner," says Miles, "Where do you want to go Molly?"

"There's a restaurant in Lake Park. I've dined there once. It's so long ago that I've forgotten but I've heard that it's still a good place."

"I know the bistro well," says Miles, "We take prospective lawyers out for dinner at the place."

"Part of the screening process," says Molly, "I bet you've had some fancy dinners."

Miles pats his stomach and grins at Molly.

"A few too many," he says.

"I like your body," says Molly, "I'm not keen on muscle men."

"That's good to know," says Miles, and he pulls her close to him again.

They kiss again and smile at each other with the assurance of mature lovers. After several moments, Miles pulls his cellphone out of his pocket and finds the website.

"There is a table available tomorrow at 7pm. Does that work?"

Molly nods and sinks back into the sofa, still surprised at the feeling she gets on being with Miles. There has been conflict in her life, and memories of the past are fading away. This present moment helps her realize that something good has arrived. Miles gets up and heads towards the door, feeling hope in the circle of chaos. He promises to pick up Molly at 6.30pm the following evening. Molly promises to wear something good because it is a special evening.

Miles drives back to his apartment, thinking about Molly and her natural charm and grace. He gets home and opens his cellphone wanting to text Molly because he misses her. He thinks about the evening with Molly. A year ago, he was holding Liv in his arms, and it is clear to him that it is over with her.

She met someone else, as he suspected. And he can't stop thinking about Molly and her quiet beauty. Her willingness to run with him, the way in which she kissed him remind him of a past carefree time, when there were no encumbrances. Impatience gets the better of him and he quickly texts her.

"I miss you," he writes.

"Same here. It was a lovely evening,"

"I'm looking forward to tomorrow," texts Miles, "Wear something nice. It's a fancy place."

"I will. I promise. Goodnight," texts Molly.

Miles looks at his cellphone wanting to see her again because he doesn't have any photographs of Molly to look at. But he has photos of Liv, and an anger stirs him to open up the photograph album.

He flicks through the photographs of himself and Liv. There are photographs of the two of them together in Puerto Rico, where they volunteered to build a home. There is a photograph of the two of them in Chicago where Miles had paid an unordainable amount of money for Liv to see the musical Hamilton.

There is a photograph of Liv with her two sons from an earlier marriage; Miles had met one of the sons and had yet to meet the other. Then, there is the photograph that she sent him that was private to them both. There is a seductive look in her eyes, and Miles remembers that they had only known each other for a few weeks. He had thought that she truly loved him in the first few weeks. Now, he realizes that it was just a mirage. Without hesitation, he removes all the photographs not wanting to look at her again. He doesn't want to see her anymore, but it might happen because Milwaukee is a village with big city aspirations.

Meanwhile, in her condominium, Liv is getting ready to go to one of her charities where she volunteers. She can hardly wait because everyone has fallen for her. A few hours later, she is making an acceptance speech.

"I hope I earn it," says Liv, with the conviction of a thousand Eve Harringtons. Liv has accepted an official seat on the board, and everyone smiles at her, with many wanting to be her. She is a million miles away from Miles and has moved onto her next crowd of admirers while Miles tries to pick up the pieces.

It takes him a while to fall asleep but when he does, he falls into a deep sleep punctuated with dreams of Molly walking with him and speaking to him softly. He wakes up and realizes that he has strong feelings for Molly, and he is unsure what to do or say. He wonders how she feels about him, and he thinks about the way her skin glowed when they kissed. It is time to test the waters.

Miles isn't the only one who is dealing with stress. The darkness of the last few months has fallen onto Molly and her daughters and Emily is sitting alone in her living room. Her caseload is light and there are no men in her life. No dates arranged or assignations: it is her and her alone. It seems to Emily that she has been sitting on the sofa for hours. Feeling frozen, she stretches her arms and stands up, pushing herself off the sofa: she feels lethargic, and she stretches again. Emily looks outside and has a deep urge to leave the apartment. It is a beautiful evening and summer is arriving.

She puts on her shoes and walks outside into the light. It is a short distance from the lakefront, and she walks down Prospect Avenue to the coffee place near to the harbor. A crowd is gathered around the café and there is a group singing. The beauty in their voices gives Emily time to pause as she hears the mixture of sopranos, altos and tenors rise above the crowd and settle in her body. The feeling of peace rests in her body, and she looks at people's faces seeing their joy because things are opening now that the pandemic is waning. Emily notices a young woman, holding a toddler in her arms and she looks at the man standing next to the woman, and she freezes because it is him. It's been several years since she last saw Alex and he hasn't changed in his physical appearance. She looks for a moment and looks away wanting to quickly leave the place, because she feels uncomfortable. She turns around and walks up the hill, her breath rising all the time, flooded with emotions. She walks into the kitchen, opening all the cupboards in a frenzied state. Finally, she finds the bottle, holding a small amount of liquid. She gets the glass out of the cupboard and pours herself a shot of bourbon. Collapsing onto the sofa, she drinks again, relishing the sweet taste in her mouth. Rushing in her brain are images of Alex and the memories of him pour back into her mind and body. After finishing the drink, she wraps her arms around herself and rocks like a baby. It hits her suddenly with the force of a hurricane and the tears run down her face causing her to bend over, her body wracked with anguish. The sobs throw her body into spasms, and she rolls onto the floor, wanting to stop but her body is not letting her stop. It lasts several minutes and when she finally finishes crying, she stands up and sits back on the sofa, stunned by her body's reaction. She looks at the bottle of bourbon and picks it up, walks into the kitchen and pours the rest down the sink, feeling a new strength in her body. She pours water into the coffee machine and makes a cup of coffee to free her body from the alcohol. An hour later, Emily is tucked into bed engaging in a deep sleep for the first time in months. She has finally cried.

The following day, Miles picks up Molly and they drive to the restaurant. Miles' hand rests on Molly's leg and she tries to relax, occasionally glancing at his hand, feeling the intimacy between them.

Miles and Molly look at the dishes on the menu and Miles looks at Molly in her dress. It is a beautiful cocktail dress that Molly chose for the evening because she wanted to look good for Miles and she watches him appreciate her beauty. Miles looks handsome in his newly pressed suit, choosing to omit a tie, giving him a look of casual elegance.

"What do you want Molly?" asks Miles, his hand moving across the table to connect with her.

"The same as everyone. A good life" says Molly.

Miles winks at Molly and they laugh together.

"I like your sense of humor," says Miles.

"I was being serious," says Molly.

"I know," says Miles.

Together, they choose the dishes from the French menu and the server smiles at Molly, enjoying her English accent. Ignoring Miles, the server tells Molly that she is visiting England this year now that travel is easier because of the decline in pandemic cases.

Between the chatter and the tasty dishes offered to the couple, the time speeds by and it isn't long before the coffee arrives with a slice of cake for the pair to share. Miles looks at Molly and feels a wave of emotion flood his body. It is time for Miles to speak to Molly about the way that he feels.

"I've been wanting to talk to you Molly," says Miles.

"That's funny because I've been wanting to talk to you," says Molly.

"Have you?"

"Yes, I feel awkward," says Molly, "but I think it's best to be honest with each other. You see, I have feelings for you. Romantic feelings. I'm not sure how you feel about me now but if you want to end the relationship, I will understand."

"I don't want to do that," says Miles, "You see, I feel the same way. I have feelings for you too."

"Well," says Molly with a smile, "Isn't this something?"

Miles places his credit card on top of the silver tray and adds a generous tip for the server.

"Let's get out of here," he says.

They drive back to Molly's house, occasionally smiling at each other and immersed in their own silence because they know that there has been a progression in their relationship, and both want to act on it. Yet they know that they need to be patient, especially with each other given all the recent traumas. Miles parks the car and looks at Molly.

"I know you want me to come in Molly," says Miles.

"I do," says Molly, "But I can see that you are hesitating."

"It's got nothing to do with you," says Miles, "I'm still working on myself. I'd like to take our relationship slow."

"It's fine," says Molly, "I understand. You've been through a lot."

"Well, so have you," says Miles.

"One of the gifts of being a therapist is that we know how to treat ourselves," says Molly.

"I can see you are getting better but don't you think it's too soon?" asks Miles

"I think it's too soon for both of us," says Molly, "We should use our common sense."

"I don't think I have any of that," says Miles.

Molly looks at him seeing the love in his face and she moves towards him. Miles hugs her close to him.

"I want to make a commitment," he says.

Molly watches him drive away, still unsure of where the relationship is heading.

"Words are easy. It's the actions that are hard. I hope I haven't messed things up by telling him how I feel," she thinks, walking into the house.

There was a lot that wasn't said. But images of the way Miles had looked at her fill her mind and she is moved by his affection. She resolves to try and sustain the relationship and not worry about what other people might think. Something good has happened that she can't reject.

Molly isn't the only one who is dealing with mixed emotions. Inside their house, Sarah and her husband Sam are sitting down in the living room because Sarah has told her husband that they need to talk.

"I have something to tell you Sam. I've made a terrible mistake."

"What has happened? Is it work?"

"Well, sort of. You see, I'm working with someone on a project. His name is Ian."

"What's happened Sarah?"

"I have feelings for him."

"You are in love with him?" asks Sam, with an incredulous look.

Sarah looks at Sam's face and doesn't say a word, watching his face shift from surprise to anger.

"Who the hell is he?"

"Nobody special Sam. I just wanted you to know. I wanted to tell you so we can try to work on us."

"Have you slept with him?"

Sarah nods and her face flushes at the memory of it.

"What the hell were you thinking?"

"I don't know. It just happened."

"I'm guessing it happened frequently."

Sarah nods again and she sits down to calm herself because she can feel Sam's anger. It is playing out just as she dreaded.

"I don't want you here," says Sam and Sarah looks at his face and feels the first embers of fear.

"I'll go to my mom's place," says Sarah.

"You have killed me," says Sam and he collapses on the sofa holding his head in his hands. Sam buries his head and wails, like a wounded animal. Sarah rushes to his side and holds him in her arms.

"I'm so sorry Sam. I've been trying to tell you for weeks. I feel terrible."

"Do you want a divorce?" asks Sam.

"No. I don't want that at all," says Sarah, "I love you. I always have. But I can understand if you want one. Given what I have done."

"Is this what you really want Sarah? You want to leave me for him?"

"I don't know. I feel so confused. Can I stay? I don't want to go to my mom's. It's so embarrassing. I feel like a complete fool."

Sam doesn't say a word. Instead, Sarah holds him, and they lay on the couch together, wondering what to do. Eventually, their eyes close and they fall into a fitful sleep with snatches of dreams, riddled with betrayal and deceit. When morning arrives, the family is in disarray, trying to repair the activity from the night before. Molly wakes up wondering if she will see Miles again and Sarah wakes up thinking about divorce. Emily wakes up thinking about Alex; a man who was incapable of loving her.

Fourteen

It is the start of the work week and Milwaukee is waking up. The city's inhabitants are getting out of bed, departing for work, ready to serve long hours in front of technology. Now that the pandemic is winding down, offices have reopened with many employers throwing caution to the wind with no expectation of mandatory masking. Sarah wakes up and all she can think of is the mess in her relationships. It is her usual time to get up for work and following her normal habits, she unwinds herself from her husband's arms and goes upstairs to the shower, washing herself clean. As she washes herself, she thinks about the risks she has taken.

Tears fill her eyes as she faces the consequences of the indiscrete moments. Feeling better after her cry, she walks into the wardrobe, flitting through the outfits and she chooses a simple blouse and skirt; the kind of outfit that her mother would wear. Sam is on call in the evening, so she tiptoes out of the house as he stays asleep on the sofa. Sarah wonders what to do and she thinks of her sister, Emily, who specializes in divorce cases.

It is early when she arrives at her office and she closes the door and calls her sister, who is just waking up after a night filled with bourbon.

"Sorry Emily," says Sarah, realizing that her sister is half-asleep.

"It's fine," says Emily, "I had a late night. Did you want something?"

"Are you free for lunch?"

The sisters arrange to meet at a local café and Emily wonders what is happening in her sister's life because she knows deep-down that it is something to do with the man that she saw her sister with. She saw the way that they looked at each other and it was obvious that they were more than just friends. Emily arrives at the café early because she has a sense that something is not right. She stands by the door, waiting for her sister to arrive and she notices a man looking at her. She glances over because he is good-looking, and she turns away when she sees his girlfriend return to her seat.

Emily watches Sarah walk across the road towards the café. Emily feels as if she is in a trance; the events of the past few days have caught up with her.

Emily shakes her head out of her reverie and the sisters find a seat to sit. They gaze at the menus for a moment not knowing what to say and it is only the server's words that snap them out of their daydream.

"I'll have the omelet," says Emily.

"The Greek salad," says Sarah.

They sit there for a moment and Sarah sighs, wanting to tell her sister everything that has happened.

"Things aren't going well between Sam and I," says Sarah, "I'm thinking of getting a divorce."

Emily reaches across the table and touches her sister's hand.

"I'm here for you Sarah. I knew that something wasn't right."

"Well, you saw me with Ian."

"Are you leaving Sam for him?" asks Emily.

Sarah shakes her head.

"It's not about Ian. He helped shine a light on the relationship with Sam. It hadn't been working for a while. Can you help me, Emily?"

"I'm here for you but you know I can't represent you," says Emily, "It would be a conflict of interest."

"Yes, I realize. I hoped you could suggest someone for me."

Emily thinks for a moment, her mind running down the list of potential family lawyers.

"There's a good lawyer in Milwaukee who specializes in collaborative divorces. It means you would negotiate with Sam about division of property. It's less adversarial. But Sarah, are you sure that you want to go through with this?"

Sarah shakes her head, looking at the food on the plate and realizing she has lost her appetite. The strain of events is taking its toll on her.

"I don't know Emily. I think I want to talk to someone about it. I don't want to see a therapist. I've done that in the past and it didn't work for me. Seeing a lawyer might help me work out what I want to do."

"Of all the people I know, you and Sam are the last people that I thought might break up. What happened?"

"Remember the man you met when I was in the bar?"

"I remember. Are you having an affair?"

"We did. I haven't seen him for a while. I see him at work."

"That's a difficult situation. It must be hard seeing him every day."

"He wants to be with me, but I don't know. I think he helped me think about the marriage and whether I wanted to stay."

Emily takes a notebook and pen out of her bag and writes the name of the lawyer on a piece of paper. She checks her cellphone for the number and writes it down. Sarah looks at the name of the lawyer, recognizing the address. It is close to her and Sam's apartment. She's glad it is a woman lawyer, but she still doesn't know what she wants. Her mind drifts to other friends who have married and now have children.

"We don't have children," she says, "Maybe that's why we are struggling."

"I often wondered why you didn't have kids," says Emily.

"We never talked about it," says Sarah, "We are both so busy at work, especially Sam. The hospital takes up so much of his time."

"Maybe that's the reason why you are having problems," says Emily.

"It's possible," says Sarah, looking at the piece of the paper again, wondering if she will call and feeling increasingly unsure.

She wonders whether Sam will forgive her or if it is possible for her to forgive herself. The affair happened and the feelings that she had for Ian, her colleague, have dissipated, lost in the spiral of events. It seems a long time since the first kiss and the conflict between herself and Sam has depleted any desire that she had for her colleague. The thoughts of how to continue swamp her and she realizes that she can't do anything right now. She needs to clear her mind.

Sarah places the paper into her bag and smiles at her sister.

"Thanks for your help, Emily," she says.

"Does mom know about this?" asks Emily.

"Yes. She saw me with Ian. She knew we were having an affair. She could just tell."

"Well, she's a good therapist," says Emily, "I've never been able to hide anything from her."

The day passes quickly, and Sarah hesitates before going home to Sam because she doesn't know what to say to him after everything that has happened. She's tried to rehearse a speech in her mind but falters each time she practices it because she doesn't know which way to turn.

The piece of paper is folded in her bag and part of her wants to rip it into pieces while the other part of her desperately wants to phone the lawyer. She opens the front door and walks into their condo: the silence is piercing, and she assumes that she is alone until she walks into the living room and finds Sam sitting upright and poised in the urban armchair, a piece of furniture that Sam carefully chose. Now that she thinks about it, Sam has made most of the choices, even for the small-scale apartment.

"Have you seen him?" asks Sam and Sarah shakes her head.

"I went to see Emily. I took the day off work. She's given me the name of a lawyer."

"Is this what you want Sarah?"

"I don't know. It's not clear to me that you love me anymore," says Sarah, "I think that 's why I had the affair."

"There was a time when I didn't love you, but now I do," says Sam.

"When was this?"

"There was someone too. She wanted to be with me, but I told her that I was married."

"Why didn't you say anything?"

"As I said, I love you now."

"Are you sure?"

Sam gets out of the chair and walks over to Sarah and takes her in his arms. He presses her so hard against him that she finds it hard to breathe. Finally, he lets her go and she steps backwards, thrown by the intensity of Sam's grasp. He walks back to the armchair and looks at her and smiles and she feels herself drawn back into his circle.

"I still feel something for you," says Sarah.

Sam looks at his watch and yawns. It is early but the events of the week have propelled them both into a fog of uncertainty and tiredness. They get into bed and Sarah wraps her arms around him wanting to feel his warmth. After a while, she moves away and stares at the ceiling and thinks about the piece of paper in her bag with the name of the lawyer pressed firm inside her mind.

Sarah wakes up the following morning and Sam is gone because he has an early shift. She walks into the kitchen and makes coffee for herself, glad to be alone so she can think about what she wants to do.

She looks at her cellphone and there are several messages, one of them from Ian. She thought it was over, but he is texting her to find out when she is coming back to work. She pauses before responding to his words that show his desire for her. Ian's text is a simple one: 'I miss you'. She wants to respond 'I miss you' too but she hesitates because of the conflict within her. Instead, she asks Ian if he is free for lunch because she knows that she needs to explain what has happened between her and Sam. Still, the uncertainty within her compels her to phone her mother, who has also texted her.

"It's not good mom," says Sarah, after Molly asks her what happened between her and Sam. She tells Molly about her lunch with Emily and the name of the lawyer.

"Does Sam want a divorce?" asks Molly.

"I'm not sure," says Sarah, "I'm feeling confused about the whole thing."

Molly comforts her daughter and reminds her to rely on her mother if she needs it. Molly is also feeling confused because although it seemed that Miles was no longer interested in her because of his feelings for Liv, he has contacted her, and the text made her uneasy.

"Are we finished?" he had typed in the text messages.

Without any thought or reasoning, Molly had responded.

"I'm not finished. It's not over for me."

"I'll come over."

"Good."

As soon as she puts the phone down after talking with Sarah, Miles arrives at the doorstep. She rushes to the door, feeling like a teenager school girl again, complete with piglets and long socks. She opens the door and Miles walks into the hallway: the two of them stand and look at each other for a moment until Miles moves towards Molly and she stands on her tiptoes while he kisses her. It is the best kiss so far because it is fueled by desire and the sudden fear of loss. Molly doesn't want to lose him. She looks at Miles and knows that he feels the same way.

"I know you can't stay long," says Molly, when she catches Miles looking at his watch.

"It's the clients," says Miles, "It's never-ending."

They kiss again and separate with Miles pulling a face of frustration to make Molly laugh. Her laugh fills the hallway, warming his body and he looks at her and it confirms his first impression that he has found a good woman: a woman very different from Liv.

"You can come back after work," says Molly.

"I will," says Miles.

"I'll be home around 5pm," says Molly.

"You have clients too," says Miles.

"Just easing back into it," says Molly, "many of my clients like the virtual sessions so I can work from home. It became popular after the pandemic."

Miles leaves and Molly tries to straighten her mind because she needs to go into the office to see one of her clients, who has always preferred the in-person sessions. The day passes quickly and when Miles returns to Molly's house, it is as if he has never left. Again, Molly feels that she knows him and that he knows her, and it is difficult to understand why unless one acknowledges the power of fate. They kiss and Molly giggles at the teenage rashness.

"What is it?" asks Miles

"I'm not laughing at you. Just laughing at myself and how I feel like a kid when I'm with you."

"I feel the same," says Miles and he kisses her again.

"I'm guessing you are hungry," says Molly and Miles nods, appreciating Molly's kindness.

"What's your favorite food?" he asks

"Pasta."

"Good food for runners," says Miles.

They walk into the kitchen and Miles sniffs the aroma from the pan filled with chicken, vegetables, and broth.

"It's simmering," says Molly, "The rice won't take very long," and she holds up a packet of instant rice. They look at each other and grin. Instant rice is a staple of single people.

"Are you fine with eating in the kitchen?"

"I grew up poor," says Miles, "That's where we always ate."

"Same here," says Molly, "my parents didn't have much money."

"You certainly did well for yourself," says Miles.

"I worked hard. I guess you did too."

Miles nods and he sits on the bench nestled into the alcove in the corner of the kitchen and watches Molly dish the meat, vegetables, and rice into the pan. There is a bottle of red wine on the table and Miles pours the liquid into the glasses. Molly sits down next to him, and they are ensconced on the bench like an old couple who have been together for decades. It isn't long before the couple finish their meal and Miles takes Molly's hand and kisses it.

"You are so beautiful," he says.

"Thanks," says Molly. "I think you are very handsome." She laughs and whispers in his ear.

"We sound so formal."

They get up from the table and Molly walks up the stairs. She glances back and Miles is just a step behind her. She walks into the bedroom, pleased that she has changed the sheets, and she turns around and embraces Miles. Miles kisses her neck and takes off her dress. It is a beautiful moment for them both because the past is gone, and they are living in the present and not caring about the future. Because of their age, there is no wildness of youth as they touch each other. They are both patient and slow and when Miles touches her body, Molly feels connected and safe. Miles lets out a cry of gratefulness that fills Molly's body and she cries out with pleasure. After it is over, they lie on the bed feeling connected to each other.

"I'm too young for this," says Molly and they both laugh at the pleasure of being together.

"You know that I love you," says Miles and they both stop laughing and look at each other.

"I feel the same way," says Molly.

"Do you love me?"

"Yes. I love you, Miles. I think I always have."

"When we first met?"

"It happened quite quickly. I tried to resist it, but I couldn't stop it from happening."

"Do you want to be with me?"

"You know that I do."

"I'm just concerned. You are a strong person. I'm worried I will drag you down. I'm still struggling with what happened to me. I'm quite weak in many ways."

"I've thought it through. I'd like to try. I think we can be good together."

They kiss again and Miles pulls Molly towards him. They pull the sheets over themselves like teenagers, who have just been caught by their parents. Miles points at the clock and they giggle because it is still early, and it is light outside. They drift into a deep sleep, punctuated by the sound of the clock, gently ticking.

Fifteen

It is morning and the light touches Molly's eyes. She blinks and smiles because Miles is there. His hand reaches out to touch her skin and she responds with a light kiss on his cheek. Feeling shy, she gets out of bed and puts on a dressing gown.

"Tea or coffee?" she asks as Miles sits up and smiles at her.

"What do you want?" asks Miles.

"The English like to drink tea first and then coffee. I'm still English in my habits."

The pair look at each other again and smile with the joy of spending the night together. Molly walks down the stairs into the kitchen and pours water into the electric kettle. The house is quiet and when the tea is made, she walks back up the stairs and into the bedroom. Miles is looking at his cellphone with a frown.

"Did something happen?" she asks

"It's one of the clients. She bought some sugar gliders."

"Sugar gliders?" says Molly, shaking her head.

"I know. From what I've learned, they are marsupials. They can glide rather than fly. She bought half a dozen."

"That seems a lot."

"She has them in a cage. I need to set up a trust for them. What do you have planned for today?"

"The usual. My regular clients and I need to check in with my daughter. She's having some problems."

"Is this Sarah? I remember when you saw her in the car. I'm sure she is grateful for your help."

"I don't know. It's a little messy. Because of the man we saw her with."

"The husband is jealous, I'm guessing?"

"It's someone from work," she says. "She's a good woman. I think it was just a mistake."

"It happens," says Miles.

He kisses Molly again and whispers in her ear that he loves her.

"I love you too," she responds.

After coffee, they both get dressed and Molly can't stop smiling because there is something about Miles that makes her blush. She wonders if it's because he reminds her of the fictional detective in her book. She also wonders what Sarah would think about Miles if she knew. She guesses that Sarah would not be happy about the sudden romance after her father's death. Emily, on the other hand, wouldn't really care because she is too caught up in her own romances.

Molly pushes the guilt to one side not wanting to worry or be concerned. She decides to tell Sarah when she sees her again. There is nothing to be embarrassed about. She is single and the marriage between herself and Michael had died several years before.

Now, she has met a man who makes her feel beautiful again. A man who wants to be with her, despite the fading of youth. For Molly, it seems unusual to fall in love at an older age, yet she can't deny the appeal and attraction of Miles. He is a man who has opened her through his touch. Molly's reverie is disturbed when Miles' phone rings. He looks at the phone and his face turns red. It seems like an era until it stops ringing and Molly freezes as she watches Miles listen to the voice message because she has an awful feeling.

"Was it Liv?" she asks.

Miles nods and sighs, unable to look at Molly.

"She found some things of mine at her place. I can go now to pick them up."

"Are you sure? After the way she treated you?" asks Molly.

"I want the things back. It's over with her," says Miles, still not looking at her and Molly feels a pit in her stomach because she thinks he is still not over the relationship with Liv.

"Do you still have feelings for her?" asks Molly.

"No. Not really but I think we should still take it slow Molly. I'm a handful for you," says Miles after he has dressed.

"I understand," says Molly, trying to hide her sadness.

"You seem disappointed," says Miles.

"I can't lie. I have feelings for you."

"I have feelings for you too. It's just after what happened, I'm not sure that I'm the right person for you. I feel so weak."

"Take your time," says Molly, with compassion welling inside her.

"You are a very good woman. I still want to see you."

"I'm glad. You know where I am," says Molly.

After he has gone, she sits on the couch, feeling sad because she thought it had been going so well. In her mind, she searches for mistakes on her part and also considers whether the romance has been too rushed. They are both grieving losses and Miles has been a welcome retreat after the death of her husband.

"I need to take care of myself,' she says, thinking about a long run along the lakefront to calm down. She looks at her phone, still hoping to see another text message from Miles but it isn't there. She casts the fears to one side and walks up the stairs to change into her running clothes.

Despite all the events that have occurred, there is one constant in her life: the running. There is a warm breeze as Molly runs along the street and heads towards the lakefront. After a mile, the conversation between herself and Miles seems a distant memory and she thinks about the time they have spent together. His words seem trivial because his actions have been constant and caring. He always shows up regardless of his mood or words of self-doubt. She thinks about herself and her actions as she runs along the path, picking up her feet like a ballet dancer who is flying across the dance floor, focused and calm. She runs down the hill that leads to the harbor, looking at the small group of people sitting outside, enjoying the warmer weather. She touches her pocket and finds her wallet and keys, reminding herself to drop in for coffee on the way back. She runs another mile and turns back around, glad to have spent the hour in sunshine, with positive thoughts of Miles and the way that he touches her. Molly walks into the store and waits in line for a coffee, wishing that Miles was with her because she associates coffee time with him. She gets her coffee and looks around for a place to sit; it is then that she sees her. The woman is deep in talk, speaking with a younger woman and Molly realizes it is mother and daughter. She recognizes Liv from a photograph that Miles showed her when he was describing the relationship. Molly freezes for a moment, because it is inconceivable that she should see Liv at this moment in time, and she curses the timing.

"I need to get out of here," she says, her arousal growing at the sight of Liv, a woman who hurt Miles.

Quickly, she walks outside with her coffee and chooses a table far away from the indoor seating, feeling a mixture of emotions. Part of her wants to quickly drain her coffee and to run back up the drive yet another side of her is fascinated by the woman inside the coffee shop; a woman who intrigues and repulses her. Molly looks at the door to the coffee shop, her anger rising and she, wills Liv to walk out but it never happens and so she drains her coffee, and gets out of her chair, determined to run back to her home and get rid of her fury.

Molly dashes up the hill, compelled by the wish to be home, not thinking of the past or the future or the possibility of being alone. She takes deep, panting breaths like a dog that is filled with pent-up energy and wishes to escape the confinement of a place.

She reaches her house and stops with her hands on her knees, bent over, trying to get air into her lungs. The street is quiet, and she inhales deep breaths, finding her way back to normalcy.

"What is happening to me?", she thinks as she walks inside the house and the place seems very quiet.

She closes her eyes for a moment imagining that her daughters are children again, running through the house with their feet thumping on the floors. Now they are grown with lives of their own. She sniffs the air wanting to smell a memory of Michael, something to make her feel like a responsible adult but it never comes. Instead, she walks upstairs to the bedroom and looks at the sheets, still tangled. She peels off her clothes, damp from the exertion, and walks into the bathroom for a shower. The water pelts her body, and she stands in the shower feeling the emotion coming out of her in short waves. She sobs for the loss and the tears prick her eyes, making them feel uncomfortable.

"I'm hurting," she cries out. The water continues to hit her body and the waves of emotion ebb. The intense feelings of anger and sadness weaken when she gets out of the shower and towel dries her hair.

Molly looks at herself in the mirror and thinks about the morning's events, rational thought taking precedence over the tidal wave of emotions. She thinks back to the sight of Liv and wonders what compelled her to feel such emotions because she doesn't know her; she only knows what Miles has told her.

"It is not my business," she says as she finishes dressing and walks down the stairs, trying to mentally prepare to see her clients. Thoughts of sending Miles a message about what happened diminish as her logical mind tells her it is something to say in person. Because, somewhere in her soul is the knowledge that she will see him again.

Molly isn't the only person whose thoughts are confused and whose body is rebelling. Sarah's world is swirling as she walks into her office, thinking about the last few days. Because she has her own office, she can close the door, and she takes the paper with the lawyer's name out of her purse. It is 8.45am and the place is quiet when Sarah calls the divorce lawyer.

She speaks with the lawyer's secretary and makes an appointment for the following week, wondering about the decision to go ahead.

She walks into the office kitchen and places a coffee pod in the machine, feeling the need for caffeine. Her phone vibrates and it is Ian.

"I need to talk to you," he says.

"I know Ian. I'm in the kitchen."

He is there in moments. She turns around to see him standing in the doorway with a look of love on his face. It is more than she can stand but she smiles at him, torn between needing affection and wanting to keep her distance. Ian tries to kiss her, but she pushes him away.

"Please don't do that," she says and is grateful when one of the other staff walks into the kitchen. Sarah blushes but the staff member is lost in a daydream, looking at her cellphone oblivious to everyone and everything. Sarah walks out of the kitchen, but Ian is right behind her, trying to get her attention. He grabs her by the arm, and she freezes, feeling his insistence and need to be with her.

"I want to see you," he says.

"It's best if we don't," says Sarah, "Sam knows about you."

Ian's facial expression changes and he looks apprehensive. But then he remembers what Sam looks like. He's thin with little muscle, unlike Ian.

"I can stand up to him," he says.

"It's best if you don't. He has a short temper."

"That doesn't bother me, but I'll go along with what you want Sarah," says Ian, "I don't want to hurt you."

"I know you don't," says Sarah, "I'm sorry about what has happened. I didn't want you to get dragged into this."

Sarah shakes her head wondering why things are so difficult at times. The look of adoration is clear in Ian's face, and she feels pinpricks of guilt.

"We can talk about it later," she says, trying to sound strong but her heart aches when she looks at Ian. She is glad that they are both at work where all the rules are in place, telling them how to behave. She looks at her watch and reminds Ian of the meeting with the research and development team.

Feeling more composed, she returns to her office and looks at her email and texts. There are none from Sam and she feels relieved because she knows she needs to tell him about contacting the divorce lawyer.

The day passes quickly with little opportunity for Sarah and Ian to discuss what is happening in Sarah's life.

"We can have coffee tomorrow," she promises, as she heads home to Sam, wondering what awaits her. Sam is asleep on the couch when she walks in, and she watches him stir at the sound of her footsteps. Sam rubs his eyes and looks at Sarah, trying to focus.

"What time is it?" he asks, and he watches the energy sap out of her.

Sarah looks at her watch and tells him the time, not knowing what to say to her husband.

"You can't even talk to me anymore," says Sam. Sarah tenses but thinks about her resolve to be honest with him.

"I have something to tell you", says Sarah, "I have an appointment with the divorce lawyer next week," she says.

Sam wraps his arms over his head and curls into a ball.

"Please don't do this," he says and Sarah rushes to him, wrapping her arms around him, "I'm so sorry," she says.

"I'm going to kill us all," he says and the fear rushes through Sarah's body snapping her back into anxiety. She unwraps her hands from Sam and stands back.

"Please don't say that. You don't mean it," she says.

Sam shakes his head, and a cold chill invades Sarah's body as she watches him get up and look at her. Sarah stands there for a moment feeling Sam's power and wanting to diffuse the situation.

"Sleep will help us," says Sarah, and the couple get into bed and Sam shifts to his favored side of the bed, turning away from his wife. Sarah hesitates before getting into bed next to him. She wills herself to go to sleep, but it doesn't happen, and she knows that she needs to get out. Her body is rigid when she gets out of bed, and she tiptoes around the room picking up her clothes, tossed on a bedroom chair. She walks into the bathroom and locks the door, making sure that Sam can't hear her. Her heart is racing as she puts on her top and skirt, just wanting to leave the house.

She walks into the living area and picks up her bag, quietly closing the front door behind her. She walks into the garage, still nervous that Sam might wake up and find her gone. The feeling of relief arrives when she drives down the road and she heads towards her old home; a place where she lived for most of her adult life. It is a place where she feels welcome, and she knows that her mother is alone.

She finds the key to the house, hidden in a safe compartment in her wallet, and she opens the door. The house is in darkness and Sarah tries to find her balance as she navigates the hallway, looking for the stairs. Slowly, she makes her way up to her old room and she turns on the hallway light because Molly's door is closed. The room is still there with her name on the door. She feels safe and she texts her mother to tell her that she is back at the house.

Sixteen

Molly wakes up in the morning and picks up her phone to see if Miles has contacted her. There is only one message on the phone from Sarah and when Molly reads the message, she gets out of bed and walks to Sarah's old room and opens the door to check that her daughter is safe. She is relieved when Sarah calls out to her.

"Is that you mom?"

"It's me. Do you want some coffee?"

"What time is it?"

"It's early. Just after six."

"I'll get up and come downstairs."

"I can bring it up."

Molly walks into the kitchen, her mind trying to wake up to the beginning of the day. She places a coffee pod into the machine and pours water into the kettle so she can enjoy a cup of tea. The normalcy of the day creates a shelter from the trauma. She makes the drinks and heads upstairs, wrapping her mind around Sarah being back home. In her old room.

"What happened?" asks Molly, placing the cup of coffee on the nightstand.

"I was scared," says Sarah, "I just needed to get out of there."

"Did Sam hurt you?"

"He threatened me," says Sarah.

"I can't believe he would do that," says Molly, "I'm glad you came here."

Molly looks at her daughter and remembers the first time that Sarah introduced her to Sam. He had been a catch, coming from a well-regarded family in the area and with a future as a doctor. They were still an attractive couple with Sam's dark and handsome looks complimenting the fairness of Sarah – looks that Sarah had inherited from her mother.

Molly thinks back to the first time that he had come to their house for dinner, and she had noticed how he had looked at Sarah, and his look had given Molly pause. It had not been a look to put her at ease because she could see that Sarah had fallen for him. It was only after he had gone that Emily whispered in her mother's ear.

"I don't like him. There's something about his eyes."

At the time, Molly had told her youngest daughter to be quiet because she didn't want conflict within the house. It was a time when Emily had been young and more conformist than rebel. It was during a time when they had been a family, held together through tradition and custom rather than sentiment. Now, the memory of the dinner is returning to Molly, and she is feeling uncomfortable again, because she knows that Emily's first impression was right.

Sarah finishes her coffee and Molly takes the cup wanting to help her daughter.

"You can stay here as long as you like," she says

"Thanks Mom. I don't know what to do anymore."

Sarah's phone buzzes and she picks it up, her hand shaking. She looks at her mother.

"It's Sam," she says, "I should call him back."

Before Molly can protest, Sarah slips into her bedroom and closes the door. Molly stands close to the door, not wanting to eavesdrop but wanting to rush to her daughter. It is all she can do not to knock on the door and intervene, but it isn't long before Sarah opens the door.

"I need to go back and talk to Sam. I left so abruptly. Most of this is my fault."

"Are you sure Sarah?" says Molly, "Don't blame yourself for this. Remember what he said."

"I don't think he meant what he said."

"Well at least have some coffee first before you go back," says Molly, hoping she can persuade her daughter to change her mind.

Sarah takes a long breath.

"You are right. I don't need to rush over there."

"I'm going to take a shower first," says Molly, "I won't be long. We can have coffee together."

Molly returns to her room, feeling a compulsion inside her. She wants to check her phone to see if Miles has contacted her but there are no messages from him, and she braces herself for the end of the relationship.

She gets in the shower and tries to wash away the feelings of rejection and thinks about her daughter and the problems in Sarah's marriage.

"How can I help Sarah?" she thinks, as she lathers her body with soap, her mind flitting from one thought to the next. It isn't long before she thinks of Miles. "I can't believe he would disappear. Disappear just like that."

She dries her hair and dresses in a casual outfit. Molly has no clients today and is catching up on paperwork. It seems like a normal day apart from the drama that is unfolding. Molly tries to cling onto normalcy, and she walks down the stairs to find Sarah making a fresh brew

"Do you want a cup mom?"

Molly nods and clutches the side of the table, feeling dizzy from all the commotion. She looks at Sarah who seems strangely calm. Molly freezes - her mind in another place - and she is snapped out of her reverie when the doorbell rings. Straight away, she knows who it is. She walks to the door and Miles is standing there.

"I'm sorry Molly. I need to see you," says Miles, wiping the sweat away from his brow.

"Come in," she says, "it's fine. My daughter is here. You can meet her."

Molly walks into the kitchen and Miles walks behind at a slower pace, feeling nervous about meeting one of Molly's adult children.

"This is Miles," says Molly and she watches Miles shake Sarah's hand.

"I'm sorry about the sweat. I was running," says Miles.

Sarah smiles politely, seeing the closeness between her mother and Miles. It is a closeness that transcends friendship. Sarah looks at her watch feeling the urge to see Sam.

"I need to head out Mom," she says, and embraces Molly. She looks at Miles and sees a kindness in his eyes.

"It was good to meet you," she says, shaking his hand.

"Let me know if you need anything," says Molly, watching her daughter head out of the door. She closes the door and turns around. Miles is right next to her, and he takes her face in his hands, caressing her, and kissing her.

"I missed you," he says, and she looks at him in earnest.

"I missed you too. I didn't think I was going to see you again."

"Why? My mess isn't your fault," says Miles.

He kisses her again and she feels the warmth from his body.

"I need to go to work," says Miles, "But I just wanted to see you."

"I'm going to work too," says Molly and she looks into his eyes, seeing the sincerity of his conviction.

"Are you free tonight?" asks Miles.

"I am. Next week, I'm taking a week off work. I'm moving into the new place before I close on the house."

"We can celebrate," says Miles.

"I should tell you," says Molly, "I had a shock. I saw Liv

yesterday."

"You saw her? How bad for you. I am sorry," says Miles.

"I was surprised at my response," says Molly, "We can talk about it later."

"That would be good. I've been thinking about it too," says Miles.

Miles opens the door, and the blast of Wisconsin wind hits him, and he laughs.

"It's always winter in Milwaukee," he says, "I'll come around seven, if that's fine with you."

Molly nods and watches him run down the road towards his condominium. The feeling of warmth stays with her all morning, and she marvels at the way in which everything is turning into something good for her. She hopes the same is true for both her daughters, especially Sarah. While Molly thinks about the day ahead, Sarah is walking into the apartment, fearing what will happen between herself and Sam. She finds Sam in the kitchen, making his first cup of coffee. It seems like a normal day only it isn't, and Sarah stands in the door way and tells him that she is sorry.

"I wondered where you were," says Sam.

"I went to my mom's."

"Why?"

"I was scared. It was because of what you said."

"Oh that?" says Sam and he laughs. "I didn't mean it."

Sarah is transfixed and looks at the floor, immobile and

numb. Sam pours her a cup of coffee and brings it over to her. Finally, she sits down at the kitchen counter and takes off her coat, feeling like a robot. There is a clock on the kitchen wall and Sarah looks at it.

The clock is slowly ticking and Sarah gazes at the minute hand, willing the time to hurry but it seems like every minute is equal to an hour. Sam's phone rings and she watches him talk into his cellphone, his eyes crinkling with laughter. Each of Sam's movements is slow, like a reel of a silent movie. Sarah looks at her cup of coffee and takes a few sips. The bolt from the caffeine wakes her up and she unfreezes, finally coming back to normalcy. She looks at her husband and wonders how it came to this. He had seemed so normal when they had first met.

"I won't leave you," she says.

"If you do, will you be with him?"

"I don't think so. He is more of a friend."

"I'm sure he likes you."

Sarah looks at the floor again, thinking of Ian's declarations of love but she decides not to say anything because she doesn't know how Sam will react.

"I don't know what to say," says Sarah. Sam takes a step back and looks at her. He doesn't say a word yet there is a message in his eyes, that Sarah finds unnerving. Sam's phone rings and he curses when he answers it.

"I need to go into work," says Sam, "there's a problem with

one of my patients."

He looks at his watch again and Sarah notices that he doesn't look her in the eye; it is enough for her to consider whether this is a lie.

"I'm going into work too," she says, "I'm still working on the project."

The day passes very slowly for Sarah and when she gets home, Sam is waiting for her again. He is sitting in the same living room chair, and she wonders where he went. He takes one look at her and decides for them both.

"Let's go out Sarah. A drink will help you."

Sarah smiles because she knows that a drink will ease her racing mind, so she agrees, relinquishing the conformity within the relationship. The bars and eateries of Lower East Side are a popular place for Milwaukee residents and when the couple walk into the trendy bar, they have trouble finding a place to sit. They spot a seat at the bar and Sarah sits down on the stool, while Sam stands close to her. Sarah feels claustrophobic and she is scared.

She orders an old-fashioned and the liquid soothes her, and she stops clutching the bar stool, relaxing, and watching the other people who have arrived for happy hour.

Sam doesn't say a word. Instead, he sips his beer and watches Sarah drink the cocktail.

"Do you want another?" asks the bartender after Sarah finishes her drink but Sarah shakes her head, not wanting to overindulge. Sam finishes his beer, and he pulls Sarah off the barstool, gripping her hand as they walk through the bar. They get outside and Sarah releases her hand from his grip. Sam whispers in her ear.

"What's wrong with you?"

"Nothing. I just don't want you to touch me."

"I'm your husband Sarah," says Sam.

"I know."

They walk together in silence and Sarah thinks about what she wants to do, slowly extricating herself from the situation. They get back inside and without saying a word, Sarah walks up the stairs into the bedroom and takes out a small overnight bag.

"I can't believe you are doing this," says Sam, following her upstairs and into the bedroom.

"I need some time alone," says Sarah and she thinks of the small boutique hotel that is a few miles away. It is a place to consider her choices and to think about all that has happened. It takes but a few moments to select some clothes and to pack toiletries. Sam disappears and she is frozen for a moment, wondering what is on his mind. She walks downstairs and he is sitting in the living area. There are tears in his eyes and Sarah feels guilty about her actions.

"I'm going away for a few days," she says.

"Enjoy," he says, with sarcasm in his tone and Sarah winces. Quietly, she slips out of the door and walks to the garage. She slips into the driver's seat and locks the door, feeling the relief in her body. She drives out of the garage and away from the condominium, relieved that she is leaving the place. After driving for a few blocks, she stops the car and takes the cellphone out of her bag. She calls the hotel and books a room for two nights. It only takes five minutes for her to get to the hotel and park in the car park. The hotel is quiet because of the pandemic and when Sarah walks into the reception area, the receptionist is looking at her cellphone with a bored expression on her face. Quickly, she puts down the cellphone and greets Sarah with a warm smile.

"I was looking at the news," says the receptionist.

"There's a lot happening," says Sarah, "especially with this new variant."

"The what?"

"Omicron. It's spreading and is more contagious," says Sarah.

"Oh yes, I think I heard of it."

Sarah changes the subject because all she can think about is a quiet room with no discussion of the future. She doesn't want to think about what might happen between her and Sam. There are also the attentions of Ian that are becoming more painful by the day especially as she feels torn by her feelings. She gets into the room, and it is small and suitable. It is the perfect place to be alone with her thoughts and she wonders why she didn't do this sooner before things got out of hand with Ian. A heavy weight of tiredness overwhelms her, and she gets into bed, little caring about nighttime habits. She falls into a deep sleep and when she wakes up in the morning, she can't remember her dreams. It is the first real sleep she has had in a long time, and she senses that her body has complained. She sits up in bed and looks at her cellphone, which has almost died. Her mother called her in the night, and she winces.

"I should have called," she thinks, and she plugs the phone into the charger, cursing herself for not thinking about all the necessities.

She knows that Molly worries about her. It had felt like a flight rather than a fight and she considers why she chose to leave Sam when there was a bed at home and a place with him. Because fear has no place in her mind or heart, she quickly dials Molly's cellphone number, unsure of what to say.

"Where are you?" asks Molly, "I was worried. Sam called me last night."

"What did he say?" asks Sarah.

"That he was concerned about you."

"I'm staying at a hotel mom. I just need a few days away. To think about what is happening."

"Are you safe there?" asks Molly, thinking about the conversation with Sam. She doesn't want to share all the details with her daughter on the phone. It merits a face-to-face conversation. The only problem is that she is not sure whether she wants to tell her daughter what Sam said to her.

She realizes that she wants to see Miles and talk to him about the matter. She knows he would understand.

"I'm fine mom," says Sarah, hesitating before she speaks.

"You can come over here. Anytime you want."

"I might go and stay with Emily. She reached out."

"Did she? I didn't realize."

"You know how she is. I think she's changed. She's been kind to me lately."

Molly thinks about her daughters and the last few months. Michael's death created an examination of the importance of relationships in their lives. The house, the job, and the publications seem trivial now. Even the mystery book that Molly has created seems like a foolish venture despite the book's release and popularity among murder mystery readers. The internal workings of the heart seem more important than the extrinsic awards.

Seventeen

The day passes quickly for Molly, and it isn't long before Miles shows up at her door. There is a small Italian restaurant in the Lower east side and Miles has booked a table for them. The place is quiet because it is mid-week and there is a notice on the door asking that all patrons wear a mask due to the sudden increase in cases.

"It's the Omicron variant," says Miles and he pulls out a mask and looks at Molly. She looks in her bag and frowns.

"I normally keep one in my bag."

Miles dips his hand in his pocket and pulls out a spare mask. Molly thanks him and places the mask on her face, feeling safe for a moment because of Miles. The conversation with Sam is still on her mind and she is aware of her anxiety. They sit down and Miles reaches across and touches her hand.

"You seem anxious," he says, "Is it about Liv?"

"Do you know?" she says, "It slipped my mind but I'm glad you brought it up. I wanted to talk to you about it because I thought it might help."

"You saw her?" says Miles and there is uncertainty in his voice.

"She's very beautiful," says Molly, "She was with her daughter."

Miles frowns remembering Liv's winning smile and how she used it to get her way.

"I think it was her," continues Molly, unsure now as she looks at Miles' face, "so you have a picture of her?"

"I deleted most of them," says Miles and he takes out his cellphone and starts scanning the photographs. Finally, he finds one of Liv and shows it to Molly.

"She's a grandmother," he says, and Molly pauses so she doesn't say anything derogatory about Liv's looks.

"She is attractive for an older woman," says Molly.

"She tends to have her hair up in an unattractive bun. I look at this photograph now and I don't find her attractive anymore. Not after everything that she did."

"I'm not surprised you feel this way," says Molly, "You met a narcissist. Be glad you got away."

"You helped me," says Miles.

"Not really. You helped yourself. I'm sure she realized that you were starting to see beyond the façade."

"She didn't like it when I stood up for myself," says Miles.

The server arrives with appetizers for the couple and places a basket of bread in front of them. Miles pats his stomach, mindful of his need to lose weight, and offers the bowl to Molly. She takes a small piece of bread from the basket and smears a slice with butter. The pressures of the week flee from Molly's mind as she carefully slices the bread in half and nibbles on the sourdough, enjoying the toughness of the texture.

"I must say," says Molly, "she didn't seem like a very pleasant person. This is just my opinion and not a clinical diagnosis."

Miles winks at Molly and she laughs. It seems a very long way from the nightmare of events.

"I love your sense of humor," says Miles.

"It's very English," says Molly. "Rooted in sarcasm and shenanigans."

"I'm very glad that I met you Molly," says Miles and he reaches across the table to kiss her. Molly blushes again as their lips collide.

"I'm glad that I met you too," says Molly, "I know you are genuine."

"I believe that I am," says Miles, "I care for you deeply."

"I feel the same," says Molly.

The main courses arrive, and the couple sit and eat, quietly enjoying each other's company. By now, they have removed their masks and feel safe because there are few diners in the restaurant; Milwaukee residents have become accustomed to cooking at home or using delivery services. They finish their meal and Molly gets up, looking at the people in the bar area, most of whom are eating bar snacks and sipping cocktails.

It is still quiet, but she is momentarily startled when she spots a young couple who have just arrived. It is the man who catches Molly's attention because he looks like Sam, Sarah's husband. She looks again and realizes that it is not him but the tension in her body causes her to grasp hold of the dining table chair.

She walks out of the restaurant with Miles and links her arm with his arm, seeking the warmth from his presence.

"Did something frighten you in there?" he asks, as they walk down the road.

"I thought it was my son-in-law," says Molly.

"Sarah's husband?"

"You do have a good memory. Sam called me yesterday. It was quite concerning. He was looking for Sarah."

"Did she go missing?"

"Well, she stayed in a hotel last night. There's been problems at home. I was troubled by what he said to me."

"Was he worried about her?"

"There was concern in his voice but that wasn't what troubled me. He implied that Sarah was mentally ill. He said that he was worried she was like her father. You see, I haven't shared it with anyone. Michael was not well mentally."

"Do you think Sarah has the same affliction?"

Molly shakes her head and looks at Miles with a concerned expression. She thinks back again over the past few months and her knowledge of Sarah. It is only the affair that has increased Sarah's anxiety.

"I have watched Sarah grow as a mature adult," she says.

"And you are a therapist," states Miles.

"Several of my clients have been victims of emotional abuse.

I think Sam was trying to create doubt in my mind about Sarah."

"Isn't that gaslighting?" asks Miles, "I've been reading about narcissism."

"It's insidious because it can create doubt," says Molly.

"Are you worried?"

"A little. Sarah has a wise head on her shoulders. I just hope it doesn't turn nasty."

Miles drives Molly back to the house, parks the car, and comes inside.

"You know I want you to stay," she says.

"Thank you," says Miles.

He looks around the hallway, realizing that Molly is leaving the house soon.

"Will you need my help?" he asks, pointing at the assortment of boxes.

"I've reserved movers to come this week," she says, "I'm donating most of the furniture. I need some modern things for the new place. It's quite trendy."

"I wish you were moving in with me," says Miles and he sees the look of surprise on Molly's face.

"That's a lovely thing to say," she says.

"I mean it," says Miles.

"I know. I probably would too. It's just that I'm something of a people pleaser. I try to keep it in check but there's part of me that likes to keep my public image squeaky clean."

Miles waves his hand in a dismissing way and Molly laughs.

"It's not a big deal. You shouldn't worry about it."

Molly laughs again.

"Spoken like a true lawyer," she says.

The couple continue to joke and tease each other and when Molly wakes up in the morning and sees Miles sleeping next to her, she feels that she has known him for decades. It seems as if he knows her too. She walks downstairs and into the kitchen to make coffee for them both, casting aside thoughts of a cup of tea because she wants to share coffee with him. She checks the messages on her cellphone, thinking about Sarah but there is no message from her. Quickly she types a message to her daughter.

"Just checking in," she writes.

A message is returned seconds later, and Molly is relieved. Instinctively, she calls her daughter, preferring to hear her voice than decipher the brief messages on the phone.

"I'm eating breakfast," says Sarah.

"At the hotel?"

"Yes. I'm going to Emily's tonight. To stay for a few days."

"I'm glad."

"Me too. I spoke to her last night. I don't want to overstay my welcome. I told her it would be three nights at the most."

"You can come and stay with me. I'll be at the new place next week."

"I don't want to do that mom. I want to find a place of my

own."

"Have you heard from Sam?" asks Molly

"A few texts but nothing important," says Sarah, feeling the tension return to her body at the mention of his name.

"He called me," says Molly, "He told me he was worried about you."

"I hate it when he does that. Trying to make me feel that I've gone mad."

"I don't think you have," says Molly, "I'm more concerned about your safety. If anything happens or he makes some threats, please call the police."

"I will. I promise," says Sarah.

It is another morning in Milwaukee with essential workers rushing to hospitals, clinics, and health facilities to treat those whose symptoms have overwhelmed them. Some organizations ignore the rise in Omicron cases and some employees rebel and stay at home to work. The world of work is changing. Ever compliant Sarah chooses to go to work but there is a part of her that is rebelling. She is preparing to get out of bed and get ready for the day when she reads the email from human resources.

Her organization decided that everyone should stay at home. A wave of relief rushes through her body when she realizes that she doesn't have to face Ian. She doesn't want to tell him what has happened. Nightmares about Sam showing up at work to confront her fade away and her anxiety goes down.

The in-person meeting before lunch is virtual and without Ian. The project they have worked on together has ended.

She is working with a new team and Emily doesn't know them very well because they are from different departments. Even if they know of the affair, there is a part of her that doesn't care about the gossip. She calls her sister to confirm her arrival the following day and is relieved when Emily tells her that she can stay for as long as she wants.

"I can pay rent," she says.

"There's no need. I earn enough," says Emily.

"I'll stay out of your way," says Sarah.

"You better," says Emily and Sarah smiles, feeling that she is finally making peace with her sister after the earlier years of sibling rivalry.

The days pass quickly, and Sarah hears nothing from Sam although the fear is still lodged in her stomach. She is cautious when she packs her suitcase, leaves the hotel and drives to Emily's place. Later in Emily's condo, the two sisters make an omelet together, sit on kitchen stools, and talk about what has happened – what has happened to everyone.

"I still miss him," says Sarah when they talk about their father.

"I didn't realize for a while," says Emily, "I miss him too. He preferred you to me, so I know you were closer."

"Are you sure?" asks Sarah, "I always thought you were a lot like him."

"I'm probably more like him than I care to think," says Emily,

"He was into power too."

"What do you mean?" asks Sarah, "you don't seem power hungry to me."

"Power is probably the wrong word. We both liked to be in control. I'm realizing that now. It's why I always break up with men first. I don't want them to break up with me."

"And here am I," says Sarah, "a complete mess. I had an affair, and I feel bad about it."

"Did you love him?" asks Emily.

Sarah runs her fingers through her long, fair hair and her face is full of regret. She thinks about all the evenings with Ian and the way in which he had looked at her. It seems in the past now but at the time it had been a wild ride.

"I can't lie. I had feelings for him," says Sarah, "He gave me something that Sam couldn't give."

"What about now?"

Sarah shakes her head, and her face blushes with guilt because of the brief affair.

"The feelings have gone. It was a short-term fling. It helped me."

Emily takes another bite from the omelet and savors the taste of vegetables. She thinks about the marriage, and she thinks about Sam, her sister's husband, and the nature of the man because he reminds her of someone, and she can't think who it is.

"When did the problems start? Was it when Sam started

working nights?"

Sarah shakes her head thinking about the years leading up to the marriage and the years after they had wed.

"He became distant," says Sarah, choosing not to talk about the details of the marriage. She tells her sister that she is meeting the divorce attorney next week.

"Is this something you want to do?" asks Emily, sensing the doubt in Sarah's mind.

"I believe so. I think I need to talk with someone about it first. Someone who is impartial. Mom gave me the name of a therapist. She's young but mom said she is good and well-respected. She treats women who are traumatized. That's probably me."

Emily frowns thinking of her own careless affairs and contemplating whether she also needs to see a therapist.

"I know I should see someone too," she says, when she sees Sarah looking at her. Emily chews another mouthful of omelet, feeling some pressure to conform because every well-respected American has a therapist.

"The problem is that I have trouble with authority. I don't like to be told what to do."

"You should do what works for you," says Sarah, "You always seem content to me. A free spirit. Like mom."

"I really should go on that vacation," says Emily, "I delayed it because of work but now I really need it. The job can get exhausting."

"Where do you think you will go?" asks Sarah.

"Mexico. I still want to go. I don't know what I want to do while I am there, but I know I want to relax and try to figure some things out."

Emily looks at her sister again, amazed that she has moved in even though it is temporary. They get on better now than when they were teenagers. And now that Sarah is here, Emily feels better. She sees the calmness in Sarah's face because she is in a safe place.

The collision of events is unnerving, and the peace is instantly shattered when there is a knock on the door and Sarah jumps because of her fear. Emily peers out of the window and watches the delivery man drive away.

"It's some new clothes that I ordered," says Emily.

"He made me jump," says Sarah and she looks at her hands because they are shaking.

"You don't need to go back to Sam," says Emily, and she remembers her old client. A man who was unfaithful to his wife and who liked to control situations. In many ways, he was like Sam because she had seen the subtle ways in which he had influenced Sarah. He also had a temper.

Eighteen

Sarah tosses and turns all night, thinking of the mess and feeling responsible for the chaos. Her sleep is peppered with fragments of reality and science fiction as she runs through a fantasy world pursued by monsters. She wakes up in a sweat and she shields her eyes as the sun pours through the windows to illuminate her face. It takes Sarah a moment to realize where she is and she stretches her body, enjoying the luxury of being alone in a bed.

The bed is small, yet it is adequate for her needs, and she feels free because she doesn't need to go into the office. She doesn't need to face Ian, just yet. She lies back on her bed for a moment thinking about Ian and it isn't long before thoughts of Sam invade her mind. Her stomach tenses as she remembers his words. She still can't believe he threatened to kill all of them, even Ian. A man that he never met. As she rests, her mind flits back to all the times that his voice was raised. Sam has scared her before, but she had brushed it under the rug not wanting to create waves. Sarah hears her sister walking around the condo, and she gets out of bed and puts on a sweatshirt because she is slightly chilled. Sarah walks downstairs coming out of her daze.

"Did you sleep well?" asks Emily, holding out a cup of coffee.

"Not really. Lots of dreams."

"You've got a lot on your mind," says Emily but she is distracted. She looks at her cellphone, her face lighting up in anticipation.

"Did something good happen?" asks Sarah.

"I just booked my flight. I leave this weekend. I got a good deal," says Emily. She shows the pictures to her sister and Sarah looks at the hotel where Emily is staying. It is Mexico and Sarah yearns to go too.

"I'm feeling some envy. Once this is all over, I'm going to go away for a while. Somewhere quiet," says Sarah.

Sarah finishes her coffee and walks into the guest bedroom to take a shower. The water rushes over her body, cleansing her face, and she wraps her arms around herself, forgetting all the stress. She's noticed a change in herself since she left Sam, but she knows that it won't be easy to get over what has happened. She gets out of the shower and dries her long hair. Once dressed, she reaches for her wallet and takes the card out of the holder. It is gone nine o'clock in the morning, and the therapist answers her phone straight away.

"I'm free this afternoon if you want to come today," says the therapist.

"My mother recommended you," says Sarah, hearing the warmth in the therapist's voice, "She's a therapist too. Dr Molly Williams."

"I've heard of Dr. Williams. She has an excellent reputation," says the therapist.

"I think you can help me," says Sarah, and they arrange to meet at 2pm.

"You can call me Susan," says the therapist.

The therapist's office is in downtown Milwaukee, and it doesn't take Sarah long to find the place. It is hidden inside a building full of organizations and Sarah takes the elevator to the tenth floor, feeling conspicuous because she is seeing a mental health professional for the first time. She pushes down the tinges of paranoia and opens the door to Susan's office, pleased to see that the waiting room is empty. Sarah doesn't want to meet any other clients, fearful of revealing why she is there. The door opens and a petite young woman comes out to greet her. Sarah is relieved that Susan is similar in age, and she walks into the office, sinking into the chair. They exchange small talk for a while, and when Susan takes off her mask, Sarah does the same. Sarah takes a deep breath and tells her why she needs help.

"It's my marriage," she says, "I think I want to end it."

"Why are you thinking of ending it?"

"I made a mistake. I had an affair."

Sarah hesitates for a moment and looks at Susan's face for reassurance because she wants to tell her everything that has happened. Susan looks at her with a warm expression and the story pours out in chunks. After she finishes talking, she looks at Susan again waiting to hear some words of encouragement.

"It seems you had an affair because you were lonely," says Susan.

Sarah nods and she thinks of all the time that she spent alone when Sam was at the hospital. The two women continue to talk. Susan encourages Sarah to talk about the marriage, the beginning, middle and end of the five-year relationship.

"At the beginning," says Sarah, "there was a lot of boom. We went on lots of dates, and he bought me many gifts. His parents were wealthy, so he was financially stable."

"Did you like him?" asks Susan and Sarah pauses, thinking of the first few months after they had met.

"It was such a whirlwind. I fell for him quite quickly because he was handsome and generous."

"You were in love," says Susan.

Sarah nods remembering the nights at Sam's condominium when he made her dinner, poured her glasses of wine, and made love to her on his king-size bed. A bed fit for a couple rather than a single man. It had felt like a Hollywood romance and when he had asked her to marry him after only a few months, she had naturally said yes because she couldn't imagine being with anyone else. He had lit up her world and so the therapist's question about liking Sam takes her by surprise because she had always loved him. Even now, talking about Sam, there is some warmth in her heart for him. The thought of ending the marriage fills her with some dread.

"I think I used to like him," she says, "But now. Now, that you ask, I'm not sure if I do."

"What about Ian?" asks the therapist.

Sarah thinks about her relationship with Ian.

"Yes, I like him. It was an affair, and I know I did something bad. He was innocent in all of this."

"It seems you blame yourself for what has happened," says Susan.

Sarah frowns and she clenches her fists, not wanting to show her anger to the therapist.

"I take responsibility," says Sarah, "But I'm not fully to blame."

"I'm glad you realize this," says Susan and she smiles warmly at Sarah. Sometimes it works to play the devil's advocate. The young therapist listens to Sarah and her eyes sparkle with kindness as Sarah slowly describes the details of the relationship with Sam. It is easy for Sarah to describe the joy of the first year of marriage, the rush to get home to see Sam and the pleasure of social events as a newly married couple. Slowly, Sarah describes the aspects of the marriage that were questionable to her and Susan winces when Sarah describes the abuse.

"I have something that might be helpful," says Susan and she gets out of her chair and walks to the large desk in the corner of the room. She flips through the materials in her folder and finally finds the chart. She walks over to Sarah and sits next to her on the couch: she shows Sarah the chart – a Power and

Control chart.

"Take a look at it," says Susan, "You can share with me your thoughts and feelings."

Sarah looks at all the segments of the chart that have group headings and examples of each phenomenon: Economic, Male Privilege, Isolation, Violence, Children.

Sarah studies the chart, reminding herself of incidents that have occurred over the last few years, before and during the marriage.

"There was emotional abuse," says Sarah, thinking of the subtle put-downs and guilt trips. She looks at Susan and knows that it is time to tell the truth, terrible though it is to her.

"He threatened me a few weeks ago."

"He threatened to kill you?" asks Susan.

Sarah nods and her body shakes as she recalls the incident.

"It wasn't just me that he threatened," says Sarah, "It was Ian too. He said he would kill us all. I didn't report it, but I probably should have done. I was so scared. He hasn't done anything."

"The two of us can create a plan of safety," says Susan.

"Thanks, but I don't really need one. My sister is keeping me safe. He doesn't know my location," says Sarah.

"It seems this is bigger than getting a divorce," says Susan.

"I think it will help me. To get the divorce. I don't want to be with someone who scares me," says Sarah.

"There are some things that shouldn't be tolerated," says

Susan.

"That's what my mom said," says Sarah and the two women smile at each other although Sarah is still anxious because she knows there is a long journey ahead. The hour is almost over, and Sarah makes an appointment for the following week.

"I will need you," says Sarah, "To help me through this."

Susan shakes Sarah's hand, and she notices that Sarah's face is calmer. Before she had come to therapy, she had already decided to leave the marriage. It was a relationship speckled with regret and fear. Sarah walks out of the office, feeling calmer about her decision. She looks around, wanting to leave the concrete jungle and she decides to take a walk by the river. She finds the path, remembering all the summers she spent with her family when she was a child, enjoying the festivals and ice cream.

She walks up the stairs to the riverwalk, stops, smiles, and laughs because on the corner is a statue of The Fonze. She never saw the show, but her father had liked it, so he watched the reruns, and she caught glimpses of the coolest actor on television. Sarah turns towards the river and the light is shining on the water, blinding her momentarily to all that has happened. After a while, she walks back to her car, thinking of the next important appointment: to gain counsel from a lawyer. She might be calm, but she doesn't know what to do because she wants to stay safe.

It is an illusion to think that life is calm because events

constantly play out again and again until people wake up to their illusions. By the time Miles and Molly meet again in the evening, both have shed their egos and are willing to be open with each other. They want to be together in whatever form it takes.

"I know this might be too soon," says Miles, "But if I asked you, would you be mine?"

"Yes," says Molly, "You know I will. I already am yours."

"I'd like to make it official," says Miles, "I'm not a louse Molly. I've just made some mistakes. Especially with Liv. I let her get between us and I can see now it was all a façade."

"I feel the same. I've experienced guilt too," says Molly, "It seemed disloyal to fall for you after Michael died. Yet our relationship seems right to me. I love being with you. You make me feel wanted."

Molly reaches across and holds Miles' hand. They are sitting in the living room and the room is empty because of all the boxes strewn across the floor. Molly is moving out of the house in the morning and the movers are arriving early. Miles points at all the boxes.

"Are you ready to leave?" he asks, "Can I help?"

"I've hired some chunky college students to load a van," says Molly and Miles laughs at her sense of humor. He realizes that Molly is making a fresh start in her life. He pulls her up from the sofa and wraps his arms around her, wanting the warmth from her touch.

"You are a wonderful woman Molly," he says.

"I love you too Miles," says Molly. They embrace and they don't want to pull away, but the inevitable call of clients and work toil taps on the door.

Miles looks at his watch and frowns because he really doesn't want to leave.

"I need to go," he says, "It's work. I have a bunch of documents to review before tomorrow's meeting."

"You are very unconventional for a lawyer," says Molly, "Not cut-throat at all."

"I never was," says Miles, "not even with Liv. Once she left me, I didn't bother her apart from when I visited her to ask her why. I respected her wishes."

"Did you go around to see her?" asks Molly, remembering the text that he got from her.

"I did but she wasn't there. She had left the items on her front door step. I'm glad I didn't see her. Or her new man," says Miles.

"I find that people like Liv move on very quickly. I'm sure if her friends had a party, they would share similar stories. There's always a polished public persona and a darker private life," says Molly.

"I'm glad I'm with you now," says Miles, "You take me for who I am."

Molly smiles at Miles and wraps her arms around him.

"Well, of course," she says, "I like you just the way you are.

You don't need to change for me."

Within minutes, he is gone, and Molly tries to focus on the days ahead because she has clients who need therapy. She feels guilty because she has been slow in returning to office life and hasn't returned all the phone calls that typically come from people who are desperate for help. Now, it is evening, and she thinks about her daughters and the turmoil that has turned their lives upside down. She wants to call Sarah but stops herself from becoming a helicopter, zooming in to untangle her daughter's problems. She reminds herself that Sarah is an adult who can organize herself and deal with mess. She walks upstairs to the bedroom, still thinking of Miles' kiss and how they came together. It seems surreal yet also realistic. She looks at herself in the mirror again and the view is of a good-looking woman. Not a stunning woman but someone who society would describe as attractive. She rubs her eyes, feeling tired after the day's events, and she peers closer into the mirror, liking the image that she sees.

"I still need to work on my self-esteem," she thinks but her bed is calling, and she doesn't want to think about it too much.

Meanwhile, feeling like a thief sneaking off in the night, Emily is checking in for a late-night flight to Cancun. Fully masked, she looks around the empty terminal, wanting to rip off the covering. She feels like an interloper with no eyeshadow, or lipstick, and she closes her eyes already feeling her feet dipping into the sand on a Mexican beach. Even though the trip was planned it still feels like a last-minute reckless fling, and it is the opportunity she needs to unwind. Because of the rise in Omicron Covid cases, the law offices are closed, and clients are grappling with technology and the telephone. For Emily, it feels like something new is starting. People are entering the airport terminal. She notices an older man with a belly look at her and she turns away, realizing that the days of casual flings are over. It was never really who she was but a reaction to loss. Losing her dad woke her up. She boards the plane and closes her eyes, dismissing the alcohol that the flight attendant is offering: It brings back memories of too many cocktails and casual men. She falls asleep and forgets the past. When she opens her eyes, the plane lands in Cancun, spring break home for many, and a tranquil place for her.

Nineteen

It is Emily's final day in Cancun, and she thinks about the five days she has spent in the land of the sun. The walks along the beach at sunrise, the first dip of her toes into the cool water, the solitary dinners in the favored restaurants in the area, and the trip to the nature park where she swam down the secret river. Men had looked at her and she had avoided their gaze, choosing to talk to older couples who were seeking respite from busy work lives. She eats her breakfast, walks back to the hotel room, and moves her suitcase out into the corridor. She slings her jacket into her oversize bag, mindful that even in the Fall, Milwaukee can be cold. Walking downstairs to the foyer, she checks out, and waits for the shuttle to take her back to the airport. She wonders about her sister, who is alone in the condo, and she feels guilty that she abandoned her. She sent Sarah pictures during the week to stay in touch. She grabs the cellphone from her bag and sends a text to her sister.

'I'm on my way home," she types.

Finally, the shuttle arrives and within an hour, Emily is at the airport, thinking about catching up on sleep during the flight. She finds the gate for her flight and sits down, flipping mindlessly through social media posts that she hasn't perused in a week. She discovers that not much has changed and wonders how the Instagram model was able to paint her eyes in such a way that there is no smudge. She glances at her watch, feeling bored, and she turns around to look at the airport official, wondering when he will make the call to board. It is then that she sees him, and she blushes, instantly drawn by the dark smudges under his eyes, and his unruly, tousled hair. She looks away because he is not her type; there is no charm in his face or eyes that sparkle at the sight of her. He is alone and comfortable with his solitude; the kind of person she wants to be. Finally, the official makes the call for boarding, and she moves into the line, glad she can afford to be a premier customer. She feels the man's presence behind her, and she resists the urge to turn around and to smile at him. She sits in the second row behind the business executive and a much younger woman, whom Emily suspects is not his daughter. She places her bag on the floor until the flight attendant tells her that it is too large and needs to be placed in the storage above the seats. She gets up and, by chance, he is standing there.

"I'm next to you," he says in a matter-of-fact way, and he opens the storage door, takes her bag, and places it inside the space, and puts his own bag next to Emily's carry-on. Emily shuffles back into her seat and the young man sits next to her.

"Sorry if I was too macho man," he says and Emily laughs, because her macho men days are behind her.

"I'm trying to let it go," he says, and she smiles. She glances over at him, waiting to be met with a dazzling smile with perfectly formed white teeth. Instead, she discovers he is looking at her as if he knows her and she realizes that he looks vaguely familiar.

"Do I know you?" asks Emily, "You seem familiar, and I can't remember if we met."

Emily hopes he is not one of the casual flings that she has enjoyed over the last few years. She waits for him to wink at her in a way that suggests an earlier encounter, but he is not forthcoming.

"We haven't really met but you know my mom," he says, "you represented her a couple of years ago. Her name is Helen Phillips."

Emily's eyes open in recognition at the name and she recalls a beautiful older woman with fair hair cropped in a pixie style. "I remember Helen," she says.

"I picked her up once after she met with you. It was the day before you went to court."

"Adam. I remember your name," says Emily.

"My mom said you were very smart."

"I have a good memory. That's all," says Emily, trying to be modest in the moment because she is looking at Adam's face and he is looking at her with an interest that she hasn't seen before. The nights of narcissistic men evaporate because somehow, she feels she is talking to someone who is genuine.

"Why were you in Cancun?" asks Emily.

"I went to see my dad," says Adam and his arm brushes against Emily's arm. She turns her head away so he can't see her blush again.

"How was it?" says Emily, remembering the stories that Helen had shared with her. The stories had been a way for Helen to confide in someone. Emily had sensed her loneliness too.

Emily had explained to Helen that Wisconsin was a no-fault state so all that could be done was a petition for divorce. Yet, she had remembered Helen's story of infidelity because of her distress.

"I'm sure my mom told you what he was like," says Adam.

Emily nods and she looks into Adam's eyes and sees his distress. Adam had paid his father a visit while Emily had dipped her feet into the sand. The experiences had been quite different, and she understands why Adam looks like he has been in a car wreck: he has visited his father, who was battling many things.

"Did he recover?" asks Emily, "I often wondered. It must have been hard for you both."

"It's been three years, and he hasn't had a single drop," says Adam, brushing tousled hair out of his eyes.

"That's a relief. Your mom told me about the drinking," says Emily.

"I'm sure she told you about the women too," says Adam and Emily nods.

"I felt embarrassed," says Adam, looking at Emily again, "I

pretended it wasn't happening."

"It must have been hard for you both," says Emily, and she accepts the drink from the flight attendant – a glass of sparkling water. She watches Adam drink his can of diet soda. Adam catches her watching him and he smiles, a genuine smile, his eyes crinkling with appreciation at the attention she is showing him.

"You are a good listener," he says, and he touches his face, realizing that he took off his mask after they boarded the plane.

"I'm sorry," he says, "I realize that I made you take off your mask."

"It's fine," says Emily, "I'm fully vaccinated."

"So am I," says Adam, "It's this new variant. It's highly contagious."

"I know," says Emily, "I felt like taking a risk. I have problems talking with the mask."

"Same here," says Adam and the couple continue to talk, moving onto other more accessible topics such as Mexico and its people.

"My dad met someone down there. Not his usual young fling but someone the same age."

"What about your mom?" asks Emily.

Adam shakes his head and sadness sweeps across his face.

"She is still recovering but she is getting better. She's just not ready to be with someone."

Adam looks at Emily and glances at her right hand again because there is no ring on her finger.

"Are you with someone?" he asks

"I was," says Emily, "but it ended."

Emily bites her lip wanting to say more but she decides not to fan any fires because she doesn't know Adam very well.

"I was with someone too," says Adam, "but I ended it because we weren't very compatible."

"How so?" asks Emily

"She was a little too far to the right for me," says Adam and Emily sighs with relief because she had taken him for a republican.

"That's good to hear," says Emily, "my mom is English. She raised us as liberals despite my dad's catholic ways."

"Your mom is English?" asks Adam, raising his eyebrows.

Emily nods realizing how she has taken her mother's English ways for granted over the years.

"We went to London when we were children," says Emily, "I'd like to go back sometime. To visit Hampton Court. I like the Tudors."

"I've always wanted to go to England," says Adam and he smiles at her again with a look of respect. Emily realizes she likes him even more and she feels conscious again because he is so unlike Ryan and the rest of the casual friends. There had been benefits yet it had all been shallow; manufactured and plastic like the shiny cars that they drove. Finally, the plane arrives back in Milwaukee, and they embark from the plane, pausing for a moment as they leave the gate because there is uncertainty in their interactions despite the words that have been exchanged. Finally, Adam musters some courage and takes the lead, as is typical of a young man from the mid-west. "I'd like to see you. Are you free for dinner this week?"

"I am," says Emily and her eyes sparkle with hope. She likes him and he seems genuine. The pair exchange phone numbers and their fingers brush as they part, not wanting to push boundaries because they have only just met.

Although she might deny the initial attraction, Emily drives back to her condominium in a daze, remembering the conversation and the way that he looked. After years in the wilderness, stumbling from one man to the next, she has met someone who brings hope. It is the middle of the afternoon when she arrives home and she gets the key out of her handbag, fumbling to open the door. When the door opens, she is momentarily surprised to see her sister standing in the doorway.

"It's good to see you Emily," says Sarah, hugging her sister, "I've missed you."

"I missed you too," says Emily, remembering the times when she wished her sister had been with her in Mexico. She had also been scared for her and had been relieved when Sarah had texted her.

"I'm on my way out," says Sarah, "I'm meeting the lawyer."

Emily slaps her hand on her forehead and shakes her head.

"I totally forgot," she says, and she reaches out to her sister to hug her back.

"I'm nervous," says Sarah.

"Just remember what you have decided to do," says Emily, "Let the lawyer take care of the rest."

It is a bright and sunny day in Milwaukee as Sarah drives to the lawyer's office and she thinks about her sessions with the therapist that have helped her decide. Talking about her feelings about her husband helped her realize that although she loved him, the feelings faded after the first couple of years because of the lack of love. There had also been the put-downs and veiled threats. They had never been severe enough to warn anyone or to tell anyone but gradually they had worn her down. When she met Ian, she had realized that she deserved better. She reaches the lawyer's office quickly and parks her car, still battling anxiety but she musters courage to walk inside.

The streets are quiet because many Milwaukee residents are shut inside, fearful of the new Covid variant with many choosing to work from home or leave their jobs, wearied from the toil of the pandemic. Sarah's anxiety disappears when she walks into the office because the lawyer greets her with a warm smile, much like the smile that the therapist offered her. She realizes that it is time to make it happen.

After the meeting is over, the lawyer shows Sarah to the door with a promise to serve the papers within the next forty-eight hours. Sarah hadn't divulged the details of what had happened and had discovered that there was no need because all that was required was the filling in of numerous forms. It had been a dull activity apart from the prospect of making the break official. The lawyer is conscientious and doesn't ask about the marriage or why it ended. Sarah gets into the car and texts her sister to tell her that the papers have been completed. The calm enters her body as she drives back to Emily's condominium, and she starts to think about the future – a life without Sam. The day passes quickly and when the evening arrives, the two sisters walk down to a local bar and drink a glass of wine.

"To freedom," says Emily and she clinks Sarah's glass.

"I need to call mom," says Sarah, "She'll be wondering what has happened."

"Mom has changed. She's a lot more relaxed lately," says Emily, "I spoke to her this week."

"She's met someone. I think that's why," says Sarah.

"Met someone? I didn't know," says Emily.

"He seems nice. He's a lawyer too," says Sarah, "I met him by accident. He came to see mom when I stayed over one night."

"She kept quiet about it," says Emily.

"Well, she's never spoken much about her private life," says Sarah, "I don't even know if she had a boyfriend before she met dad."

"I'm sure she did," says Emily, "She's English."

The two sisters laugh. Unaware that her daughters are discussing her romance with Miles, Molly is slipping into a summer dress because Miles is taking her out for a night at the cinema. She checks her bag to ensure that she has the mask ready and checks her wallet to make sure that her inoculation card is inside. The doorbell rings and he is standing there. They stroll down to the Oriental Cinema together, buy tickets, and walk inside.

The film is showing in the largest of the three screen rooms and they sit close to the back, watching other fully masked seniors walk in. Molly relaxes in her seat and looks at Miles. He winks at her and slowly takes off his mask because there are only six people in the entire cinema. It is time to relax and enjoy the movie. Miles holds up the large box of popcorn and offers it to Molly, who takes a handful and pops it into her mouth.

She holds up the large container filled with soda and slurps through the straw, feeling like a child again. She offers the container to Miles, and he smiles at her, thinking of the time that they first met in the coffee shop. So much has happened with so little time to take a deep breath and relax. They watch the advertisements on the screen and the list of donors who enable the cinema to keep working during the pandemic. The film begins.

Twenty

It is a year later and a beautiful spring day in Milwaukee. The couple are standing in their garden, and they smile at each other, feasting in the delight of each other's presence. The garden is small and perfect for the day, with the first buds of spring peeping their way from the ground to welcome the start of a new time. It is a new time because Miles and Molly are getting married, and they can't quite believe it is happening.

Molly pinches herself and giggles like a schoolchild because there is something magical about the way that

Miles looks at her and the way that she looks at him. Molly looks at Miles and realizes that his eyes are full of tears, and she strokes his face with such a look of tenderness that Miles brushes the tears away, realizing that the moment has arrived. "You are such a wonderful woman," he whispers into Molly's ear.

"I'm so lucky to have you," says Molly.

They are alone in the garden, waiting for the guests to arrive and Molly sighs with relief that the only people attending are family members and their partners. Miles checks his phone and shows Molly the text message that he has received from his son.

"Jason is running a little late," he says with a frown.

"There's no rush," says Molly, "The service doesn't start for another hour."

"I'm glad I put you in charge of this. You know I'm not good with organizing," says Miles.

"I tried to keep it simple," says Molly, "I didn't want a lot of fuss."

"I know," says Miles, and he squeezes Molly's hand again, taking in her beauty and the simplicity of her dress.

She looks very beautiful to him and for a moment he considers his narrow escape from Liv. If he had married Liv, it would have been a life of servitude, devoted to meeting her every need and whim. He sighs again relieved that he hasn't seen Liv, and he is glad that she doesn't travel in his circle. When he compares her to Molly, it is like comparing night with day because Molly is giving and independent; the perfect woman for him. Molly looks at the garden again and is glad that the arrangement for the wedding is simple and refined. It is perfect for Sarah and Emily, her daughters. Sarah arrives first and there is no ring on her finger but there is a look of contentment that Molly hasn't seen in several years. Molly can tell that her daughter is better and is enjoying her time alone.

"How's your new place?" she asks Sarah, kissing her lightly on the cheek.

"It's wonderful mom. It's a small building but I've met some people. My neighbors are quiet."

Ten minutes later, Emily and Adam arrive at the house and Molly kisses her daughter, making sure not to squeeze her too tight.

"The monster is complaining today," says Emily, patting her stomach.

"I'm so excited for you both," says Molly and she hugs Adam with affection. The doorbell rings again and Molly looks at Miles.

"It must be Jason," he says, looking at his watch and realizing that, for once, his son is on time. It is one of the most important days in Miles' life and his heart is melting at the sight of Molly. Miles walks to the door and opens it, taking in Jason's new girlfriend and he sighs with relief because she doesn't look like the other ones. There is no vacant stare in her gaze and no signature tattoo on her arm.

"This is Jenny," says Jason and the young woman shakes Miles' hand. Her grip is firm and there is a kindness in her eyes that reminds Miles of Molly.

"Thanks for inviting me to your wedding," says Jenny and the couple step into the hallway. The door is still ajar, and Miles watches a car arrive at the house and he realizes that it is the officiant. His heart leaps into the air because it is almost time to marry Molly. He walks into the living room, followed by his son and Jenny. Molly rushes to hug Jason, whom she has met several times, and he introduces her to Jenny.

Miles sees the look of relief in Molly's eyes at the sight of

Jenny. Molly glances at Miles and smiles in a way that makes Miles love her even more.

"I'm so happy to meet you at last," says Molly, and she grips Jenny's hand. There are no narcissists present at the private event. The officiant is a firm and kind woman who calls everyone outside because it is time for Miles and Molly to marry. Molly feels slightly dazed and giddy because she still can't quite believe that she is marrying Miles and when they join hands and he slips the ring onto her finger, the feeling of love increases. They are in unity.

"Congratulations," says the officiant and the couple embrace, enjoying the moment of betrothal. Their children circle them and embrace them. Both of Molly's daughters have tears in their eyes because they appreciate that they have a new father. Jason looks at Molly and he embraces her and the hug between them is different. The group walk into the living room and Molly speaks to the officiant.

"We have food and a cake," she says.

"I need to go but thank you," says the officiant, "I've got another one in an hour. The pandemic stirred people to get hitched, so I've been busy."

The spread of food is laid out on the large dining room table. There is a variety of small plates encompassing cuisine from Italy, Mexico, America, and England.

"Are those pork pies?" asks Jenny, peering at the table.

Molly laughs with joy because it is rare for an American,

particularly a young woman, to be aware of this English delicacy. Molly watches Jenny place one of the pies on her plate and then spoon a spoonful of salad next to it.

"Have you been to England?" asks Molly

Jenny nods and bites into the pork pie with a look of relish on her face.

"I went during my senior year. It was an exchange program. I lived near Battersea."

"One of the nicer parts of London," says Molly.

Molly looks up from her conversation and Miles is smiling at her with the humbleness of a newlywed. Instinctively, she walks towards him and kisses him on the lips, not caring that their children are all in the same place. In fact, none of them really care because they are so caught up in the moment that everything seems perfect.

There is no look of loss in Sarah's eyes or any desire to find another to replace. Molly moves towards Sarah wanting to find out what is happening in her life because the visits have been infrequent since Sarah moved to the new apartment.

"Are you still loving your new job?" she asks her daughter and Sarah's face lights up with joy.

"It's wonderful. I'm my own boss. No micro-management. Just an opportunity to do some research. I work mainly on my own."

"Have you made friends yet?" asks Molly.

"Yes, but not at work. I joined a running group. I'm training for a race with them."

"That's wonderful Sarah. You motivate me to run more."

They walk into the kitchen and Sarah looks at the cake that her mother has bought for the wedding. It is a simple cake, laced with chocolate and vanilla. It is the perfect dessert for the couple and Sarah picks up the cake and carries it into the living room. Miles and Molly pick up the knife and slice the cake in half, revealing the white buttercream inside the chocolate exterior.

Miles cuts again and places a small part of the cake onto an English plate decorated with trees and birds.

He holds up the plate and spoons a piece of cake into Molly's mouth. She bites into the cake, relishing the flavor, and wipes the buttercream away from her lips, savoring the taste of the delicious cake. The family members gather around, and each takes a slice of cake, tasting and enjoying the richness of the sponge.

"I'm happy for you dad," says Jason and he hugs Miles, clasping him in his arms, remembering the troubles that Miles has experienced.

"I'm the lucky one," says Miles, "I really appreciate you coming today. It means a lot."

Jason looks at his watch and tells his father that they need to leave because they need to visit Jenny's mother.

"She is getting out of hospital today. She got Covid but she recovered."

"That is a relief," says Molly, joining in with their conversation.

"Where are you going on honeymoon?" asks Jenny and Molly smiles because it is a very simple vacation.

"A tour of Wisconsin," says Molly, "I've lived here for thirty years but there are places I've never seen. Miles has planned the itinerary."

"I'm switching off my work cellphone," says Miles, "One of the other lawyers is looking after my clients while we are gone."

They slowly leave, wanting to stay yet acknowledging that Molly and Miles want to be alone. Finally, it is just the two of them and they walk into the bedroom, acknowledging that it is different this time. They are married and there is a sparkle in their eyes.

"You stripped down quickly," says Miles and Molly laughs because she still enjoys Miles' sense of humor.

"I love your body," says Molly.

"Do you?"

"Yes, every inch of it."

The touch is familiar yet unique when they glance at each other's ring. Miles strokes Molly's face and sighs in a way to show appreciation of the woman that he met and now has married. Molly smiles at the sight of Miles and she touches him with the joy of a new love. They take their time in enjoying each other and when it is over, they stay in bed and hold hands.

"I love you," says Molly.

"I love you too," says Miles and he remembers his old relationship. He knows he shouldn't, but he can't help himself.

"What are you thinking?" asks Molly, looking at his face.

"I'm remembering Liv. She said that 'love is fleeting'."

"How do you feel about her now Miles?"

"I feel I dodged a bullet," says Miles, "Our relationship is very different."

"She's an interesting person. A classic narcissist. Very textbook," says Molly.

"Do you miss Michael?" asks Miles.

Molly looks at Miles and shakes her head.

"I'm very glad that I met you," says Molly. "I feel close to you." She looks at the ring on her finger and strokes his face again.

"I'm glad we are married," she says, and they kiss, enjoying the contact and the mellowness of their age. They sleep through the night and when they wake up, the light is pouring through the window. The week stretches before them as they contemplate a new life together.

Molly gets out of bed and puts on a robe, relishing the thought of bringing Miles a cup of coffee even though she has made him coffee so many times. Today, it is different because they are together, and it is different because they have made a promise to each other. She walks downstairs and into the kitchen, placing the granules in the coffee pot. She smiles when Miles walks into the kitchen.

"I planned to bring it upstairs to you," she says as he wraps his arms around her.

"I want to drink coffee with my new wife," says Miles and the joy in his face creates a stirring inside her that is visceral and real. Molly looks at the clock, mindful that it is a Monday and that they don't need to go to work. They sit at the kitchen table, sipping their coffee and looking at each other. They are lovers who are on the verge of new adventures. Time is on their side.